Times and Tides

by

Janet Gogerty

Dedication

Colin Gogerty for his cover work and technical support

To Cynthia and all at Hinton and Library Writers; great story tellers and listeners.

To Jane and all at The Spokes for listening

To all the regulars at Author Chat Forum for support and encouragement

To Alex for keeping me faintly in touch with reality

To Cameron and Erin for keeping the fiction flag flying

and in memory of Evelyn

Table of Contents

Preface

Enjoy twenty five stories in alphabetical order starting with a blind date and ending on Xmas Eve, with no clue as to what you might expect in between.

Most of the tales were written for our weekly writing group; our themes are always interpreted with such variety the direction any story takes is based on personal experience and wild stretches of imagination. In this third collection of short stories are some real places and experiences plus much that could happen or should never happen.

Some of these stories have been previously published in anthologies, on line or on my website.

Blind Date

Jessica hesitated at the door of the restaurant. Why had she let herself be talked into another blind date after the last two disasters, someone else Di knew from 'The Centre'. Jessica was a few minutes early and sat nervously at the table the waiter offered her.

Di hadn't mentioned that her blind date actually was blind and she was taken by surprise when he arrived. Jessica had no objection to meeting men with disabilities, on the contrary, they were likely to be more interesting. She knew from Di's work that you can't categorise people, registered blind did not necessarily mean a world of total darkness, but as Michael entered the brightly lit restaurant he looked genuine. His guide dog led him in, the waiter greeted him and chatted for a few moments before carefully leading him over to the table where she was sitting.

As he sat down opposite her and she saw how gorgeous he was, she knew he would not have given her a second glance had he been sighted. He smiled and as she automatically smiled back, a whole host of questions came to mind about the practicalities of this date, but he was at pains to put her at her ease. He spoke in a rich baritone.

'I've booked a cab for seven o'clock, it's not far to the concert hall. I've already consulted the waiter about the menu, but please take your time choosing.'

'Thanks, I can never decide and lots of the dishes...' she faltered, wondering what her voice sounded like to him, hopefully interesting and sexy 'look... uhm sound delicious.'

He laughed. 'Jessica, you don't have to avoid saying 'look' or 'see'. I'm lucky I haven't always been blind, I like people to describe what they are seeing. Tell me about the décor of this place and see if it matches what I imagine. Tell me about the other diners, but not loud enough for them to hear.'

Now she noticed the scarring, it made him look more attractive, but it seemed rude to ask what had happened. Army probably, already she had romantic visions of herself as the strong wife helping him to regain his life, going to The Palace with him to receive his medal.

'Are you okay?... If you're quiet I won't know if you're still there, it's not unknown for a date to slip quietly away.'

'Oh I wouldn't do that, well not till I've had my dinner' she giggled.

A smile crinkled his scars, he had a sense of humour.

The concert was a good first date idea in case conversation ran dry, but they found it easy to chat.

'How long?'

'Four years; I have no sight at all, accident in the lab. I'm determined to finish my masters' degree, 'the centre' has been a godsend with the specially adapted computers and of course I couldn't do it without the help of Bella.'

'Bella?' She felt a stab of jealousy.

'My dog' he reached down to pat the animal lying quietly by his side.

Jessica thought Bella was not a name that suited the dog, but presumed her beauty was on the inside. 'I thought guide dogs were usually Labradors?'

'She is part Labrador,' he said defensively 'Bella's the best thing that's happened to me since the accident. Anyway, enough about me…'

The moment she always dreaded, there was little to tell; not a lot to say about the office and her favourite hobby, photography, seemed a no-go area, but somehow she found herself telling him of wandering around London, snapping people unaware of her presence. Natural shots of lives lived frenetically or barely at all. The blanket and the bench; the woman resting on the flank of the sleeping dog, who in turn lay on the reclining body of his master; the trio sheltering under a blanket, unaware or immune to the bustle around them.

'That's beautiful, you've conjured up your pictures for me, I don't need to see them.'

At the concert hall it was a full house, their seats were right at the front so there was room for Bella to stretch out.

'I hope you won't get a stiff neck craning up.'

'I haven't been to many live concerts, I'm enjoying watching what's going on. There's a very tall bloke with a tiny violin and a tiny girl perched on a stool with a double bass twice her size.'

Michael laughed, the evening was still going well. Either side of them people smiled and commented on the dog. He was happy to let them chat.

Very brave you lads... good to see you out and about... they give you free tickets don't they... marvellous these dogs, does he empty the washing machine as well?

Michael whispered in her ear. 'It's often like this, I just smile and nod.'

She stifled a giggle. Now they were sitting down she could see Bella properly and the dog stared back, her lip slightly curled. The creature never stirred during the first piece, her head rested on her paws and she kept her adoring gaze on Michael, except for sideways glances at Jessica.

As the orchestra left the stage at the interval Michael said 'Take my arm the other side from Bella, I don't want to lose you in the crowd.'

Bella paced herself and her master in the slow shuffle up the shallow steps of the aisle. Michael had pre-ordered drinks at the bar and said 'Excuse us' politely, but confidently.

'If you hang back, you never get to the front.'

Jessica popped to the Ladies while Michael took the dog outside.

'We'll meet you back at our seats.'

'Will Bella find them?'

'Of course.'

There was a queue at the Ladies and as she came out she heard a ding dong and a voice saying *Ladies and Gentlemen, would you please take your seats for the second half of tonight's concert.*

Michael and Bella were already seated.

According to the programme the second half was a long symphony Jessica did not know, with the third movement famously recognisable from a film she'd never heard of.

'Shall I read the programme to you?'

'No thanks, I already downloaded it as a pod cast so I could talk intelligently about the music.'

'Good, because I don't understand the programme notes.'

'I didn't understand the pod cast, but that should not stop us enjoying the music.'

He was right, Bella slept through it, occasionally opening one eye, but the music was thrilling. As the conductor turned to bow the audience erupted into wild applause, there were cries of bravo and some stamped their feet. Michael's face wore an ecstatic expression.

'Thank you for coming along Jessica.'

'Thank you, it's been a wonderful evening.'

She wondered if there would be another.

In the foyer his watch beeped. 'Cab's coming in five minutes, Joe, one of my regular drivers. We'll drop you off home, or if it's not presumptuous would you like to come back to my flat for coffee? I feel more comfortable on home territory and Bella can go off duty. Joe's on duty till midnight so I'll call him back as soon as you want to go home.'

Two rules of first dates; don't let him see where you live, well he couldn't, but he would hear her say the address. Second, don't go back to his place. She could slip down to the tube station or across the road to the bus stop; Jessica had done her pre date research.

'Yes, I'd love to come back for a quick cuppa.'

A blind man must be quite safe, if he came on too strong she could always slip away, but she felt as if she knew him well already.

The flat was ground floor, with the entrance round the back; there was a little garden that Bella was now racing round like a puppy.

'Sorry it's so dark, I don't need lights.'

Inside he found the light switch easily and strolled around like a sighted person. The little lounge looked bare, but what use would he have for books and pictures?

A series of barks announced that Bella was ready to come back in.

'I'll put the kettle on while you and Bella get to know each other.'

Rattles and muffled noises came from the kitchen, but no crashes of broken china as one might expect from a blind man, especially if he was nervous on a first date.

Jessica found Bella's stare unnerving. The dog's ears twitched as she followed Michael's progress without needing to look. Jessica reached out her hand, then patted the dog's head. Bella bared her teeth and without warning sank her teeth into Jessica's ankle. For a moment she was too polite to utter a sound, hoping the dog would let go and Michael be none the wiser. Bella was so perfect he might think she had accidentally put her ankle in the dog's mouth. But as the dog tightened her grip she cried out in pain and tried to push her away.

Michael rushed in and seemed to know what was happening.

'Bella off,' he shouted angrily 'this is your last bite, back to Waggy Tails rescue for you tomorrow.'

Her ankle throbbed hotly as Bella slunk past Michael. He followed her and Jessica heard the door slam.

'Jessica, I'm so sorry.' His put his arms around her. 'Is it your ankle?'

'Yes, it's okay.'

'Is it bleeding?'

'No, no, not much blood, it's just the shock, a bit of bruising.'

His closeness was taking some of the pain away, but she felt she should make some sort of protest. 'Has she done this before?'

'Well... a couple of times, I thought she'd been provoked, she's such a gentle dog, perhaps I was blind to her faults and now I suppose asking you out again is out of the question?'

'Not totally out of the question... if you get a Labrador next time.'

Michael could not see her expression to know if she was joking and Jessica did not like to ask if he really intended to send Bella away.

'Can I see you again Jessica?'

Blue and Grey

My first school was blue and grey, the only point of colour the red pinafores we wore for painting. The buildings were grey, the windows and doors blue. The school was called 'The Blue School', my uniform was blue and grey and in my class was a boy called Peter Grey. Only the name of the school is a fact. The rest is memory and conjecture. I have one tiny black and white photograph of me in my new dark grey and light grey school uniform.

I did not remember a boy called Peter Grey, but in my hand I held a letter from New Zealand stating that he was in my infants' class in 1958, a grey boy from the black and white fifties.

Dear Mrs. Compton,

I hope you will forgive this intrusion and agree that a letter is the politest way to introduce, or rather reintroduce myself...

'How on earth did he find my address or know my married name?' I asked my husband Simon, who was finally roused to interest.

'If you don't remember him he could be a conman.'

'The old fashioned kind who doesn't know how to use the internet?'

He laughed. 'Just throw it away.'

'I am curious, he's doing family research, thinks his grandmother lived underneath us.'

'So why doesn't he come to England and find out?'

'He is,' I looked at the calendar and the clock 'he's arriving at Heathrow any moment now.'

'He won't want to come up to Lincoln to track you down.'

'He's got a cousin in Gainsborough, his only living English relative; he's put the cousin's address and his email.'

'Don't give him yours Linda, or our phone numbers… don't contact him at all.'

'He knows our address, the cousin might drive him over.'

'Okay, just write to him with what you know and he won't need to bother us again.'

'He hasn't actually been any bother yet and he sounds genuine, but I know nothing about old Mrs. Denby except that, to quote my mother, she was 'a wicked old cow' who made her life a misery.'

I decided to email Peter Grey, the sooner he knew I could not help him find his family, the better.

Curious to receive your letter, but unable to help. I was an only child and my parents are deceased. We left London when I was six. P.S. I don't remember a boy called Peter Grey!

I received a rapid reply.

Thanks for your message. I don't remember a girl called Linda Wilson, but I do recall our first teacher Miss Whore, probably not spelt that way, a frail girl called Stella with only three fingers on each hand and Susan with a funny leg! Just arrived at hotel after impossibly long flight, tomorrow up to the cousin I've never met. I would value any tiny snippet of memory about those black and white days.

If you wish to meet in Lincoln for coffee on Friday (in broad daylight, bring a friend or hubby for safety, I won't be offended!), then email me back. Otherwise ignore this message and thanks for your time. Peter.

He had a sense of humour and sounded polite. No impostor could make up those details. I was curious and emailed him back.

Susan was a polio victim, my mother told me to be nice to her. Eleven a.m. in front of Lincoln Cathedral, I'll wear my bright pink anorak.

I told Simon.

'Eleven a.m. outside the cathedral? I'll be at work.'

'You'd only be bored, hearing about my infant school days.'

Peter Grey had a grey beard and would be wearing a blue anorak. I saw several men fitting that description.

'Linda? Got to get my breath back... Cousin Anne is down the bottom shopping, told me the best way to appreciate Lincoln was to walk up Steep Hill.'

'I thought New Zealand was hilly?'

'Not our part, but Anne was right, what an amazing town.'

'City, it has a cathedral and a castle. Shall we go in the Refectory?'

'What?'

'The cathedral coffee shop.'

We were soon talking about school; little Linda Wilson was another person, but when the memories returned it seemed like yesterday.

'Because we emigrated to New Zealand when I was seven,' said Peter 'that first part of my life has stayed sharp in my memory.'

'Same with me, Dad worked for Ordnance Survey and we moved quite often, so I recall my life in segments.'

'Miss Whore…'

'H A W E?'

'However she spelt her name, she was strict.'

'I used to be dragged the whole mile from home crying, with the promise of Robin comic if I was good.'

'Second year we had Miss Randall, she was ancient, but motherly.'

'Dad took me round to her house one summer evening, I thought teachers lived at the school, but we went up tall stone steps to a big black door. Inside the hall was a huge chest of drawers; she told me to open the top drawer, I pulled the gold handles, but it was impossible. Then she opened up the side, the dresser was a fake; the little door revealed steps down to a cellar. I thought that was so exciting.'

'… and in the cellar was a door out to a little garden with a rabbit in a cage. I was allowed to play with him and then she gave me milk and biscuits in this huge kitchen.'

'You went there as well?'

'But tell me about your house.'

'Didn't you ever visit your grandmother?'

'I never met her.'

'My parents called it 'the flat', they rented the top half of a large Edwardian house. The front was neat, tiny garden and a door with coloured glass.

Inside we went straight up the stairs and the house rambled back with steps and landings into three storeys. Mum had to lean out of the kitchen window to hang the washing out on a pulley line that went all the way to the end of the garden.'

'What if the line broke?'

'I guess it never did, luckily. The back garden went with the downstairs flat; Mrs. Denby never invited me to play in her garden.'

'We could both have played in the garden, I had nowhere to run around, we lived in those white flats with green windows on the main road.'

'We used to pass them on the way to the park or the river for 'fresh air and exercise', but it would have been nice to have a little boy visiting, I had no one to play with.'

'We're creating an alternative past… did you ever go in Gran… Mrs Denby's flat?'

'No, it must have been tiny, no bathroom. She was allowed to come up to our flat once a week for a bath, part of the rent agreement, but our bathroom was primitive; the hot water came out of a terrifying 'Geyser' that spluttered. But it was the fifties, everything was different then, I always think of it in black and white. No that's not true, I had a good childhood, Mum and Dad took me out and about. I think of those times in red and green, red buses and green parks.

But the house was strange. My bedroom was at the back, up the top stairs, down a long corridor.

Mostly I was too scared to get out of bed, but one night I crept to the window. I could see the lights of the backs of houses, a mirror reflection of our own terrace. I heard a child crying, saw a light go on in a top room. Then the most melancholy cry, just a cat, but it was the loneliest sound in the world.'

'You're giving me the creeps' he laughed.

'Sorry, I'm nattering on, but what can I tell you? I skipped home one day ahead of Mum, Mrs Denby's fat foot was stubbing out her cigarette butt on the doorstep. Lovely black, red and white tiles and there was that horrible ash. When Mum arrived Mrs. Denby said 'Look what the postman did.' As soon as we were upstairs I told Mum the truth. To my surprise she believed me, that was the first time I realised grown ups could lie. But surely your mother told you about your grandmother when you were grown up?'

'She said we were best off without her and thanks to Dad she didn't ruin our lives as well.'

A sudden memory came. 'Peter, I think I saw your mother once… in our kitchen, a woman with blonde hair, crying. I didn't understand, shocked to see an adult weep.'

'Mum had blonde hair; sometimes Dad looked after us because Mum had to go out. I wonder if she was looking for her father.'

'Wasn't he dead?'

'Another mystery, I'm trying to find out what happened to him.'

'It's all so long ago, but I remember Mum and the neighbour talking at the gate.

I thought she was a widow.
No, she put him in a home.

So that was him, knocking on the front door?
*Yes and look at the state he was in, all filthy
and neglected.*

That night when my father came home, mother
related the story, forgetting I was listening. It must
have all happened when I was at school.

So then the police came and took him away.
Sooner we move out of here the better.

But that doesn't mean it was your
grandmother's fault, maybe he had a mental illness.'

'In later years Dad told me he took us out to
New Zealand to get Mum away from her, said she
was a wicked old woman.'

'Is Cousin Anne from your father's side?'

'Yup, Dad left his own family behind, but he
never regretted going out there. They had three more
children. In some ways we were two families, the
younger ones had such a different beginning from me.
My mother hardly talked about the old days, but when
we started having kids and she saw Dad holding his
grandchildren, she started dwelling on the past. She
vaguely remembered her father, her mother just said
he was away. Other children's fathers had been away
during the war, so she took it for granted. But he
never came back and she assumed he was dead, too
scared to ask her mother.'

'You mustn't take what I told you as gospel. I
don't suppose anybody in our road really knew
anything about Mrs. Denby.'

'After Dad died Mum was devastated, she
became obsessed with the past. New Zealanders can
go on the internet these days, look up family history
in the old country. Mum thought it would be easy to

find out about her father. He was born, he married, he was on mother's birth certificate, then nothing.'

'I can understand how she would fantasise that the lost father was a great deal nicer than a dreadful mother.'

'It's too late now, she died last year, but the kids were fascinated by then.'

I was getting restless; this trip into the past was interesting, but it was time to wind things up. I was expecting him to tell me that his wife had died of cancer last year, or he had just gone through an acrimonious divorce.

'I expect you'll be wanting to meet up with your cousin for lunch…'

'They won't want me hanging around, my wife was looking forward to a shopping trip. She thought I should do this bit on my own, said it would be a bit full on if we all turned up and you would feel obliged to invite us all round for dinner!'

'All… how many of you?'

'Just our younger son and daughter, the others have got the kids, can't go travelling.'

'Look Peter, it's none of my business and I have to go now, but why don't you just enjoy the holiday with your family, isn't it too late to rake up the past?'

'That's what my missus says, but now you've given me something to go on.'

I stood up to go, put out my hand, but I felt a responsibility to welcome the family to England. 'If your wife would like to, our two families could meet up for lunch at the weekend, email me.'

That evening there was an email. I broke the news to Simon.

'Shall I ring Kate and Tom? It would be nice for the young ones to meet up. I didn't give him our phone number, we're going to meet them at The Quays.'

'You don't remember each other from school and now we're having a family reunion! Did you ask him how he tracked you down?'

'No.'

The cousin lent them her car and lunch went well, Peter insisted on paying. Simon enjoyed hearing about New Zealand, the restaurant was busy and the past was not discussed. Kate and Tom took the young ones off to show them around.

'Time we were going, nice to meet you Marian' said Simon. 'By the way Peter, how did you track down Linda?'

'Linda, you never mentioned your parents getting mail from New Zealand, but when Mum died we found letters from your parents and Miss Randall the teacher; we could track the family addresses, news of your marriage, your father's death... '

I was startled. 'My parents never mentioned they knew anybody in New Zealand, let alone receiving mail.'

'But your mother was not one for hoarding things,' said Simon. 'Remember how tidy her little bureau was and the sideboard drawers.'

'She always was tidy and knowing she had limited time she left everything in order... but if what Peter says is true and she was secretly receiving letters, she could have written without me knowing… but why? She was such an ordinary person and if she had friends in New Zealand why did she and Dad never visit when they did their little bit of travelling?'

We were interrupted by my mobile phone, it was Kate calling, Peter's son wanted to know when they had to return to Gainsborough. They were already half way up Steep Hill and wanted to visit a real Old English pub.

'Look, if we give you directions, come back to our house for a cup of tea, Kate and Tom can bring them back home.'

Peter looked at Simon. 'Look mate, we wouldn't want to intrude, we have rather landed on you.'

Marian spoke. 'It's nice of your daughter to show our two around and kind of you to invite us. All I ever wanted was a nice holiday to Britain, I never believed Pete was going to find your family, I think he should leave the past alone.'

'I quite agree,' said Simon 'I'm more than happy to show you around while you're in Lincolnshire and I've enjoyed hearing about New Zealand, but I don't think it's right to delve into Linda's parents' past. If they did have secrets to hide, which I'm sure they didn't, we must honour their privacy.'

'But do come back for a cuppa and see the garden' I added.

We waved them off from the car park without mentioning our car was at home. We did not live far away.

'I was expecting you to suggest we get in their car,' grinned Simon 'or were you worried Peter might be a secret axe killer?'

'I was worried we'd get involved in a marital dispute, now they can just drive away and forget about us.'

'…and what about their kids, they've just arrived in the country, no mobile phones, they're using our house as a rendezvous point…'

'I like them, it's just like meeting another couple on holiday and getting on well.'

'It could be hours before Tom and Kate bring them back, but seriously, I don't want you to get involved, we have no proof of what he said and what is he trying to prove, that he's your long lost brother?'

'You are intrigued, admit it,' I clasped his arm. 'He would have to be a twin, we must be the same age, but I see no resemblance to anyone in my family.'

We had underestimated their navigational skills and Peter and Marian were already knocking at our door.

'You should have grabbed a lift' said Peter when we explained.

'We wanted to walk off that big lunch.'

'You don't live in the castle then' he laughed.

'Bit above our price range, the historic quarter' countered Simon.

They enjoyed looking at the back garden. Peter followed me into the kitchen when I went to put the kettle on.

'I hope I haven't annoyed your husband.'

I glanced out of the window. Simon was showing Marian the greenhouse. That gave me a few minutes.

'Marian loves gardening' continued Peter, as if he had read my thoughts.

'Peter, just tell me what it is you want. If you have read the letters then don't leave me in the dark.'

He took out his wallet and removed a photograph wrapped in cellophane. I gasped. For a second I wondered how he had obtained a picture of me.

'It's Mum on her sixtieth birthday, proof we all turn into our mothers.'

He laughed. 'I recognised you straight away outside the cathedral.'

'Strange, because mum always reckoned I took after Dad's side of the family, I had his darker features.'

'Your mother was fair, like mine? But you agree you are your mother's daughter?'

'Of course, you didn't come all the way from New Zealand to tell me I was adopted, that you're my twin?'

'No, I just wanted you to be sure before I show you the letter.'

I felt a tremor of excitement and glanced guiltily out of the window; Marian was admiring Simon's vegetable beds. But it was my mother not his and I wanted to read the letter. I took the envelope from him, but paused.

'It was the last letter, that's why it looks new' said Peter.

It was my mother's handwriting, the date, the winter before she died.

...so here I am still writing letters while the rest of the world is emailing, but this will be my last letter, nothing dramatic to report, I could go on for a few more years, but I think we should stop corresponding while our grey matter is still working. Rest assured I will take our secret to the grave. My only regret is I didn't thank Miss Randall, she couldn't have picked better parents for me and she was a great help finding us somewhere to live when we were newlyweds. She could not have known how unsuitable your adoptive parents would prove to be. But you have been blessed with a large family and did the right thing getting away.

It's true what they say about getting old, the early memories return so vividly. They were happy days, why should we deny that. It was always summer, my mother was a princess and your mother beautiful. You coming round to play tea parties in our garden, was it really so vast, rolling lawns? Our fathers coming home, so smart and tall in their uniforms; your Dad used to swing you round till you were dizzy and mine would pick me up in one arm and little Dexter in the other...

The handwriting had become gradually illegible. 'Dexter? Can't read the name, but a little brother?' I sat down on the kitchen chair. 'I don't understand any of this, were both our mothers adopted? During the war, were our mothers friends, was their teacher Miss Randall? Both their families killed in air raids? With all the confusion of war she must have bypassed social workers or whatever they had then and found a nice childless couple. Parents often didn't tell their children they were adopted in those days. Mum was born in 1937, always said she was too young to remember the war. They got married when she was only seventeen, had me straight away. If she found out she was adopted I can imagine her not wanting to hurt her parents feelings and if it was never spoken of then she couldn't tell me.' My hand was steady as I poured the water from the kettle.

'A lovely story and the adoption part is true, but if you look, the boy's name is Dieter, not Dexter.'

Before I could take in the implications Simon and Marian were at the kitchen door. I slipped the letter in a drawer.

'How old is Kate?' said Marian, as we took them into the living room.

'Nearly thirty.'

'How long have they been married?'

'They're not,' said Simon 'saved us a packet.'

'They don't believe in marriage' I added.

'Might change their minds when they want kids.'

'Peter…' Marian frowned at him.

'They're not going to have babies' said Simon.

It was my turn to frown. 'We don't know that for sure.'

'They've made it pretty clear it's not going to happen.'

'Sorry,' said Marian 'didn't mean to pry. Is there a problem?'

How did we come to be discussing private family business with complete strangers?

'We have no idea if there's a problem, I've never put any pressure on Kate, I know what my mother was like. Originally she urged me to have a life, not rush into babies, then gradually came hints about not leaving it too late.'

I was hoping the young ones would return soon. Would we keep up small talk or should I insist on knowing where my mother came from, what happened to the little boy.

'Dieter, a German name. Were our mothers brought over with the Kindertransport? My mother was fair, but perhaps she was half Jewish?'

'No, the complete opposite' said Peter. 'Let me get something from the car.'

I fetched the letter and handed it to Simon.

'I'm so sorry we have landed this on you,' said Marian. 'It's our eldest, he's a journalist and historian. He started doing research after my mother-in-law's death, published it in a New Zealand history magazine, so it's unlikely you've seen it.'

MISS RANDAL; INFANT SCHOOL TEACHER, SPY, HEROINE... read the words on the front cover. I handed the magazine to Simon to read first, hoping to placate him. Despite his misgivings he was soon absorbed. He paused only to show me a picture. Confronted with the old photo I recognised her instantly. He turned the page, another black and white photograph; an anonymous smiling SS officer with his family in the garden, it could have been the scene described by my mother.

'So Peter, are you saying your mothers were intended to be the Master Race, their parents the finest 'Aryan' specimens, brought up in the countryside away from the war. Miss Randall with the ideal inside job for a spy, a nanny?'

Peter became animated. 'Yes, she must have genuinely loved her charges, innocent children. What was going to happen to them when the end became inevitable? Goebbels had his family in Hitler's Bunker, poisoned all six of his children before he shot his wife and himself. Can you imagine doing that?'

On Monday morning I was alone, the radio on, Faure's *Dolly Suite*, 'Listen With Mother'. I was transported back to the cosy Fifties, listening comfortably with my mother in our warm and safe flat. She wasn't English or any nationality, she was not young or old, she was just 'Mummy'. Did Dad know?

Tomorrow Peter Grey's son was flying in to Heathrow, meeting publishers and television people. Miss Randall had smuggled the children out, schooled them to forget, organised their lives. On Sunday night Kate told us tearfully it was certain she couldn't have children. What did it matter who her great grandparents were now, my little family had come to an end. Why couldn't I let the past rest? A grey and white picture in my mind of a man in uniform, holding a pretty girl and a little blonde boy.

Blue and Grey was first published in 'An Eclectic Mix Volume Two' AudioArcadia.com 2015

Carats

'Life is too short to spend any more of it with you' I said to Brian, as I handed back my engagement ring with its large diamond.

I immediately regretted my impulsive action and kept my eighteen carat gold wedding ring firmly attached to my finger. But I did not regret my words or my decision to leave.

Brian looked gob smacked, to use a phrase he would comprehend.

'But I don't understand.'

'Precisely' I replied.

I didn't expect to see Brian or the diamond ring again. The wedding ring fetched a reasonable price at one of those WE BUY GOLD shops, enough to pay for a break at a rural retreat. I was determined to enjoy the two weeks annual leave that I would not now be spending with Brian observing steam trains in Somerset. A whole fortnight to contemplate what I did want to do with the rest of my life; no one knew where I was and nobody at the retreat knew who I was.

At Hurlingham Hall we enjoyed eating delicious meals with interesting strangers and pondering which courses and activities to participate in each day. The choice ranged from creating Celtic jewellery to carving walking sticks, crystal healing to mystic yoga, music appreciation to writing crime fiction and in the beautiful grounds, guided walks and canoe lessons.

Television, computers and mobile phones were banned and I had no idea what was happening back in Felton. We all forgot about the outside world until one morning our coffee break was disturbed by the crunch of car wheels on the gravel driveway and interrupted by the appearance in the drawing room of two plain clothes police officers; a female sergeant and a young male constable.

I was shocked that it was me they wanted to speak to and as I accompanied them to the privacy of the library I could hear the excited murmur behind me. I could think of only one reason why they had tracked me down, but I didn't imagine Brian had the gumption to do that.

'Mrs. Belinda Anne Beresford?'

For a moment I forgot that was me, at Hurlingham Hall I had become Bella.

'Yes… has something happened to my husband, ex husband?'

'Can you identify this ring Madam, it was found at the scene of a crime.'

I was tantalisingly close to being reunited with the valuable ring, sparkling even through the clear plastic evidence bag it was sealed in.

'It is, was, my engagement ring, has something happened at our house, has something happened to Brian?'

'We won't know until the body has been identified' said the young constable.

The older woman sergeant frowned at him then spoke to me.

'Can you please confirm that you reside at the address registered on the electoral roll, 27, Graylands Avenue, Felton.'

'Yes, I mean not any more.'

'And can you confirm that Mr. Brian James Beresford also resides at that address?'

'Yes, we decided on an amicable separation ten days ago.'

'We were unable to contact him at his home address, nor at his place of work, his manager said he was away on holiday.'

'Yes, we had a holiday booked.'

'...and was he of sound mind the last time you saw him?' interrupted the constable.

'Of course, no one is of sounder mind than Brian.'

The sergeant turned aside to speak to the younger officer, I could not hear what she was saying. My brain was working overtime, I had more questions to ask than the detectives.

'Sergeant, are you saying my ring was found at the scene of a death, where did it occur and how did you know it was my ring?'

'Could you please tell us first where your husband was planning his holiday?'

'Ex husband.' For some reason I decided to withhold information. 'I have no idea, he'd booked a cottage somewhere near a railway line... look, will you please tell me if you think he is a suspect or a victim.'

'That is what we are trying to find out. There was a brutal murder at a flat behind Dingly Parade, West Felton. During the thorough search some items were removed as evidence and a jeweller observed your ring was of a unique design. We traced the shop where it was bought four years ago and where you also have it insured. You have identified it and have made no claim that it was stolen.'

'I don't know that part of Felton, nor does Brian, but I do know he could not be a murderer, he's much too boring for that. Please let me identify the body, so at least I know he's not the victim,' I felt a growing unease '...unless it was suicide.'

'No, that is one point we are certain on' said the constable with relish. 'The body was found in five separate pieces' he concluded, before the sergeant could silence him.

'Would you like a drink of water Mrs. Beresford, is there anyone you would like to call?' said the sergeant. 'I must emphasise at this stage we have no lead on who the deceased may be, no missing person reports. The best we can do to help you at this stage is to obtain DNA samples from Brian's relatives... are you okay, shall we call a doctor?'

For the first time since I left my husband I felt a twinge of guilt.

'He has no relatives, he was brought up in care, I was his family.'

A stronger pang of guilt; it wasn't just me he was upset to lose, but my whole large welcoming family. He had wanted us to have a family of our own of course, but I had pleaded there was no hurry for a baby.

I wasn't listening to what the two officers were saying and then they were gone and two matronly

29

looking members of the retreat were offering me a cup of tea and resisting the temptation to ask what was going on.

'The police are coming back this evening when they have more information for you dear, would you like someone to stay with you?'

'No, I think I'll pop up to my room.'

I sat hunched on the edge of the bed and cursed myself for not realising the obvious, not telling the CID visitors. I was rather galled that he had acted so swiftly, but Brian must have sold the ring. The events at the unknown address had nothing to do with us.

But who had he sold it to? There were no shops in Felton boasting signs WE BUY DIAMOND RINGS. He could have sold it to a mate in the pub, but he never went to the pub and I wasn't sure he had any mates.

I was indignant to think that some idiot had conned Brian out of the ring, probably for far less than it was worth, and then had the cheek to get himself murdered and cause all this trouble. Or perhaps he was the murderer, poor Brian, in league with the underworld...

An image of a little boy lost came to mind and I realised that was what had attracted me to him in the first place. His early proposal and the welcoming arms of my large family had swept us both up the aisle.

When I confessed recently to my mother that I was bored, she retorted that if I had four young children to look after like she did at my age I wouldn't have time to be bored. Then she suddenly softened and put her arm round me. *Is everything alright dear, you know I don't like to pry.*

I had assured her all was well in that department, it was the intellectual stimulation that was missing.

There was no more time to ponder, I had to act, and the only way to find out if Brian had been chopped to pieces was to go to the holiday cottage and look for him. I knew where it was, the only place we ever went on holiday.

I hurried to catch the daily mini cab that took retreat visitors to and from the station. It was a long way to Somerset and I arrived at the little single track railway halt on the last shuttle of the day. The two carriage diesel operated infrequently, when the heritage steam train was resting in its shed near the originally named 'Railway Bank Cottage', where Brian should be staying.

When he opened the door he mistook my expression of relief at finding him in one piece for the thrill of being reunited.

'Belinda, I knew you'd come before the fortnight was up...' his look of childish delight turned to an expression much darker. 'I've got something dreadful to tell you.'

I kissed his cheek, at least I was here to look after him.

'It's okay, I know what's happened, I'll make you a nice hot chocolate and we'll work out together what to do.'

'No, it's too late, I'll never find it again… I sold your engagement ring.'

'Oh Brian, thank goodness…'

'I don't understand…'

'It doesn't matter, let's not bother calling the police till we get back to Felton… are they steaming tomorrow?'

Darren's Day Out

Darren's face was pressed against the bus window as they came to a halt. Today they were visiting a new place and he hoped it would be more exciting than their usual visits to 'the shops'. Darren trailed behind his mother and the double buggy down a busy street. He could hear her talking to him but he wasn't listening, the familiar words washed over him 'Stay close blah blah don`t upset the blah blah or I'll blah blah. His heart sank as they entered a shop and were soon engulfed by racks of clothes taller than Darren.

Now his mother's mobile rang and deftly she answered while putting the baby's dummy back in, wiping his sister's nose and rummaging through the clothes. Darren looked back at the doorway, sunshine and fresh air beckoned. His only thought had been to step outside for a few seconds and jump back in before he was missed. Just one, two, three steps and look around, peer through the archway, perhaps go through…

He wanted to run into the empty space in front of him. A long path, wide grass, a huge grey building. He ran and ran then jumped down steps, turned a corner then stopped, astonished. In front of him was the largest door he had ever seen, dark and old. He felt scared; only a giant would have a door that huge. He turned to run away but was gently swept up by a little crowd of jolly looking grown ups and children. They had found a special small door cut in the big door. Perhaps the giant had been killed and it was now safe to go in.

Inside he gasped and blinked, a musty stillness wrapped around him and he gazed up and up. He knew this place had been here for ever. He stood motionless and watched the other people as they tiptoed around looking in awe. Everyone had come to see what the giant's house looked like. Now they were gathering around a bearded man wearing strange long robes. As Darren peered through legs and bags and coats at him, he realised he must be a Wizard; he had made them safe from the giant. The Wizard was telling everyone a story and Darren strained to hear and understand the grown-up words 'built by Norman'... Well that didn't seem a very scary name for a giant thought Darren; maybe he was a friendly giant. Now the Wizard pointed to large black gates with a gold padlock. Perhaps the giant wasn't dead, just captured. There was strange curly writing on the wall next to the gates and Darren couldn't pick out any words he knew from his reading book. That must be the spell to keep Norman the giant safe.

The Wizard now pointed upwards and all eyes were raised to the most beautiful window Darren had ever seen. Deep blue and red lights were shining from it and there were lovely pictures of other Wizards and strange people. The little crowd moved on but Darren stood engrossed in the pictures until he felt his bones begin to rumble and heard a low noise getting louder. His heart was beating faster; was Norman the giant speaking? The other people didn't seem surprised and smiled as the rumbling turned into music and Darren thought it was the best music he had ever heard and even louder than the stereo in his uncle's car. The music filled all the great space of the Wizard's Hall and he felt carried along with it.

Now he saw a wooden door creak open and out filed boys in white robes. The smallest wasn't much taller than Darren and had glasses and red hair. As he passed by he dropped his book and Darren saw the open pages had strange lines and dots among the words. So they must be junior wizards carrying their Spell Books. As they arranged themselves on rows of wooden seats, another adult Wizard appeared and waved his wand! They began to sing their Spells and the ethereal sound sent pleasant shivers down Darren's spine. Now he had forgotten the world outside and the Great Hall of the Wizards was everything and he couldn't bear to leave it. A plan half formed in his mind and he went to the wooden door which stood ajar. Inside he could see more robes hanging up. All he had to do was go inside and put a robe on and he would become a boy wizard too.

ooOOOooo

Amanda was not enjoying her first day as a police constable. Chaos reigned in the interview room as she tried to comfort the young mother; the baby was crying and the toddler was racing round the room.

'I only turned my back for one second and there he was gone' wailed the mother.

Amanda tried to pat her shoulder, in between leaping up to stop the toddler putting her sticky fingers on tape recorders, files and sheaves of important paperwork. Amanda's colleagues were out searching the city centre, while here at the police station, urgent calls were being made to useful networks such as Shopwatch. As the clock ticked and the hands moved round relentlessly there was still no news; Darren's granny and aunt were on their way.

Suddenly the door swung open to reveal a relieved looking inspector.

'It looks like we have found him and he's safe and well, in fact he has been thoroughly enjoying himself.'

The young mother's face lit up with relief then darkened in annoyance 'Wait till I get hold of him, where is he anyway?'

'At the cathedral, seems he wanted to join the choir; do you often go to the cathedral?' asked the inspector.

'Cathedral! Why would I go to the Cathedral?' she replied.

'How was he found?' queried Amanda.

The inspector laughed 'The choir school only just rang, they didn't realise they had an extra boy till they had nearly finished tea. He's running around in the quad with the other boys now, but one of the masters is keeping a close eye on him; we have a car waiting so you can take Darren's family there right now.'

At the choir school, while Mr Jenkins waited with Matron for Darren's family to arrive, he told her his idea.

'It could work, he seems a very bright boy and it would fit in well with our Inclusiveness Policy, it would certainly help get that government grant.'

A police car pulled up and Mr Jenkins was soon ushering Darren's mother through the archway and the gate marked 'private'. Reluctantly Darren tore himself away from the other boys and raced over to his mother.

'Mum, Mum I had a great time, we had a party, can I stay here, can I have a Nordition?'

Darren's Day Out won second prize in the Doris Gooderson Short Story

Competition 2011 and was published in the Wrekin Writers' Anthology 2011.

Energy

I didn't believe in ghosts; surely the scenes of great tragedies or terrible massacres would be filled with the presence of unhappy spirits? Or perhaps those souls have no wish to stay? Equally, I regarded with amusement stories of lone spirits helped to 'move on'. If there was an existence after death, why would souls freed from their bodies be so dependent on the earth bound?

But what of spirits with no desire to move on; glad to be rid of decrepit bodies, but loathe to leave the places they love, those in whom the spark of life has not quite been quenched, who find the energy to keep going. For there is energy all around us; from the electricity in a bolt of lightening to the electrical pulses in our brains, or the Sun, the life force that makes a plant erupt from a tiny seed. But I'm going off at a tangent; I have never been a thinker, not a spiritual person, nor a poet and certainly not a scientist; I can only relate events as I experienced them.

I inherited a country cottage recently from my Aunt Beth. You might imagine a thatched roof and roses, a dear aunt who doted on me, but the truth is more prosaic. Aunt Beth had bought the end of terrace 1930's council house in the Thatcher Years. Her parents had moved into the newly built house on the edge of Lower Middleton, relieved to give up the tumble down tied cottage. That row of old cottages, knocked into one and renovated, is now worth a fortune.

We went to visit when we were young, but were never invited to stay; three children rampaging round her precious garden and a brother-in-law she disliked. Mother and I went on duty visits over the years; I promised Mum I would not forget Aunt Beth.

She never seemed particularly pleased to see me; even if expected I was greeted with 'I was going to do the runner beans today,' or 'It's my turn to do the teas at the church hall.' Any suggestions I could help with the interrupted activities were brushed aside.

But I still felt guilty when the solicitor's letter arrived announcing her death, it had been too long since my last visit. When I rang my brother and sister with the news they replied that they thought she was already dead.

I wasn't surprised she had remembered me in her will, I presumed she had no one else to leave it to. The house and more money than I would have imagined came at an opportune moment.

My husband had announced that he was leaving me; or rather he wasn't leaving, but thought we should have an intelligent uncoupling.

'Do you know how ridiculous you sound,' I had retorted 'why don't you just tell me if there is another woman.'

There was another woman; neither of them had enough money to set up a love nest, or the courage to tell her husband. Up until his announcement I had thought we were happy, I had pictured pleasant holidays when he retired in a few years, followed by shared enjoyment of grandchildren.

Released from pretence, he spent more time with her, but still he did not leave. So I left; while he was at work. I did not leave a note to say where I had gone; but I doubted he had taken in the news of Aunt Beth.

My daughter, our daughter Zoe, was looking forward to coming with me at Easter to inspect the cottage. When she arrived in the car her father had bought her for university she was astonished at the sight of suitcases and even more astonished at my news.

'Mum, are you mad, the place is a dump, let's just go home this evening.'

'We could find a bed and breakfast, perhaps this place will look better tomorrow after a clean and tidy up.'

Zoe's face wrinkled in disgust. 'You can't sleep in the bed she died in.'

'She didn't die at home, she was found in the field by a walker.'

'At least the house won't be haunted,' she giggled 'but seriously, you can't live here, in this village, you don't know anyone and you don't like the countryside.'

'I shall, look at the view; I wonder now if I assumed I didn't like the countryside because my mother always said she couldn't wait to get away from here and then your father always wanted to go to Spain on holiday. As for the house, it has a lovely garden.'

'You don't do gardening.'

'I could learn, watch those programmes.'

'But there isn't a television.'

'I'll join the library.'

'You never go to the library.'

'I've always been too busy, now I have all the time in the world.'

'Next thing you'll be taking up knitting.'

'Maybe; I have to reinvent myself… I can't believe your father didn't tell you what's going on.'

'You're talking 'divorcespeek', why can't you call him Dad. Does he know you're coming here? Who else have you told?'

'Nobody, not even your brother.'

'I can't believe my mother has run away, suddenly I come from a broken home?'

'Blame your father for that.'

'…and work, you could be reported as missing.'

'I couldn't face telling anybody, the sympathy from the married ones and the divorced welcoming me to the sisterhood? As for work, I've posted off my resignation, I shan't miss that place.'

'Okay, let's be practical. Did Aunt Beth leave you enough money to live on?'

'Enough to do up this place and enjoy a break until I find a little local job.'

We sat in the Middle Maid Tearooms with homemade cake and Zoe's notebook. The staff were happy to help and very curious. One of them rang across to the pub which had rooms vacant, while the other brought leaflets for local tradesmen.

It was so obvious and so simple, house clearance, plumber, electrician, decorator; start from scratch. I started laughing.

'You know that lovely kitchen shop near us, it always made me want to throw everything out and start all over again with rainbow plastic bowls and Mediterranean crockery, now I can.'

The pub was comfortable and the breakfasts hearty, Zoe decided to call my bluff, we wondered how long it would be before her father or brother rang her. My mobile phone was switched off and sitting in a drawer at my former home; I couldn't face receiving calls from anybody.

At the house we found little to show it had once been the home of my grandparents and mother, we put a few photos and items in a box file in Zoe's car. There followed a procession of vans and blokes, our new friends at the tearooms had told us next door was empty, next one along abroad and another worked long hours in town. If anyone further up the road had noticed the activity they did not come to investigate.

But the work did not proceed without incident, we wondered if the men of Middleton were accident prone. The House Clearance Undertaken van had hardly gone a hundred yards up the road when it had a flat tyre. From their body language we guessed the driver and his mate were not happy, but I had paid them generously to take everything away.

The plumber emerged from under the Belfast sink with blood spurting from his hand, Zoe fetched the first aid kit from her car.

He insisted we keep the sink, back in fashion, all the basics were fine, call him again when I wanted a washing machine plumbed in and central heating installed.

The gas man slapped a red warning sticker on the gas fire and we added electric heater to the shopping list. The electrician only took two seconds to decree we must have the whole place rewired; it was dangerous and how could anyone survive in the Twenty First Century with so few sockets. He returned with his mate the next day and we extended our stay at the pub.

We found a garden centre where I ordered an elegant shed and they promised to remove the lopsided pile of wood and cobwebs where Aunt Beth kept her tools.

On the day the electricians were due to finish we retuned from town to see an ambulance drawn up outside. The electrician's mate emerged, ashen, from the front door.

'The power was off, don't know what happened, it was like he had some sort of fit.'

'Does he suffer from epilepsy?' asked Zoe.

'No, fit as a fiddle, the paramedics asked me all that.'

I was relieved when the electrician walked out unassisted.

'I'm fine, I don't want to go to hospital, we're only half an hour off finishing the job... and I don't want to spend another day in this place.'

We sat in the garden and waited till we were called to inspect the work.

'If it comes to a bit more than you quoted, that's okay,' I said 'was there a problem?'

'No, no all fine,' he said evasively 'sorry about the drama.'

When the decorator came the next day he decided to paint the outside first and give the plaster a chance to dry where the electricians had channelled into the walls. The house seemed larger now it was bare and I wondered if I could change my mind about colours. I was just putting the kettle on for his coffee when I heard a muffled yell and a thud. Rushing outside we found the ladder on the ground and the painter in the bushes.

'I'll be darned, not a breath of wind, that's never happened to me before.'

By the time Zoe had to go back to university the house smelled of new paint and I had basic furniture, with more due to be delivered, carpet on order and a land line. Our feet tapped on the bare floorboards as we admired the transformation.

'I could get a nice rug for now, to go over that patch where the pot of paint got knocked over.'

'Yes, he was rather a clumsy chap,' laughed Zoe 'but he did a good job in the end; are you sure you can manage to put the curtains up… and you'll be alright spending your first night here alone?'

'Of course.'

But as she drove off it hit me that I was alone. The past days had been busy and fun, but this wasn't a doll's house and it wasn't a game any more. I stared at the silent phone. Zoe had promised not to give anyone my number, tell them I was fine if they asked, but I would decide who to contact.

That night the house was silent, earlier in the evening there had been the sound of birds settling to roost and the house itself seemed awake.

I slept without dreaming and when I woke up knew exactly where I was, it seemed my sub conscious had drawn a line under my old life.

I trotted down the stairs to try out my new toaster, the sun was streaming in the window; it wouldn't take a psychologist to work out that settling in would have been a lot harder in the grim short days of winter. But it was strange having an unplanned day ahead, the first of many such days... I went out into the garden.

The door of the new shed was open, it had a stout catch firmly in place yesterday and I imagined a country tramp sleeping in there. The garden centre men had left the rusty tools, with their grey split wooden handles, in a neat pile by the hedge. So I was surprised to see a spade propping open the door. As I stepped in, someone rushed out past me, but there was no sign of anyone in the garden; not even a shadow. The stress of the past weeks was catching up with me.

I stood looking over the low hedge at the peaceful fields, the footpath to Upper Middleton veered away at this spot and for a moment I thought I saw a walker coming towards me. I heard a skylark and spotted the tiny dot in the sky; until the painter had pointed them out I had known nothing about the birds.

hereabouts

I thought I heard a voice and turned, it was going to take a while to get used to quiet country life.

That morning I headed up the footpath, smiling as I climbed over the stile. As children we had thought it very adventurous to get this far, but looking round I had not come far at all.

As the ground rose higher it became drier and easier to walk, but my rural idyll did not last for long. When I reached the pretty village and the little church I could not miss a bright yellow poster that filled the church notice board.

SAY NO TO FRACKING

A few yards further on I saw a man hammering a post into his colourful flowerbed, it bore the same notice.

'Good morning, I'm new in Lower Middleton, by the field.'

'Batty Beth's old house?'

I was taken aback; that he presumed to know where I lived and that he should refer to her in those terms.

'How do you know?'

'There's only one person new in your village and my son did your plumbing.'

'She was my aunt.'

'Don't worry, you don't look like her.'

'This fracking, is it over the other side of your village?'

'No, in Middle Meadow, those fields you just crossed.'

'But surely they can't do that?'

'Private land, always has been, public footpath. The landowner kept quiet, he can let them on his land, but he doesn't own what's underground.'

'What's in it for him, I don't know anything about fracking, but no one seems to want it near them.'

'Perhaps he's looking to sell the land, but even if it never happens the land will be ruined just by them testing the site,' he gave his post another thump to illustrate his anger 'disturbing the nesting skylarks… there's an emergency meeting in Lower Middleton this evening.'

With my new interest in the countryside I was roused to remark 'Why doesn't the government investigate natural sources, solar power, the sun is the source of all energy.'

He looked at me strangely 'You know then?'

Before I could answer he seemed to glance over my shoulder and I turned, but there was no one there.

'Beth will be watching over the meadow, that's for sure.'

I shivered despite the sunshine. 'What do you mean?'

'She's buried in the churchyard, by the side gate to the field, closest she's ever been to the church, but we didn't tell the new lady vicar that.'

'I didn't come to the funeral.'

'I know.'

'We didn't hear till a month later.'

'She left no instructions, not the most sociable person, no one knew who to contact. Born in the village she was entitled to one of the few remaining plots, lower churchyard is full. A month later the solicitor is renovating the office and finds where his predecessor put Beth's will, turns out she wanted to be cremated and her ashes scattered in the field.'

I shuddered. 'I should go to the churchyard.'

'You won't find a stone, that's for the relatives to provide, I do a bit of woodturning, I had a nice piece of yew for her.'

I went in through the lychgate, as I walked the narrow path I thought I saw someone slip out of the side gate. On the grassy mound was the carving.

Bethany Jane 1935-2014
May the sun always warm you.

What strange words. My family didn't do cemeteries, quick dispatch at the crematorium… I looked up but there was no one there.

I'm sure you are expecting me to say I saw an old lady wandering the meadow…

As I walked back I heard the skylarks and I heard a girl singing. As I walked past a large oak tree a girl stepped out, for a moment she reminded me of Zoe at junior school. But no, she had plaits, a summer dress and a Fairisle cardigan.

She smiled, then skipped away out of sight.

I felt surprisingly calm as I walked back to the house, as happy as that girl had looked. When I got indoors I went to the box that Zoe had remembered to take back out of the car at the last moment. I thumbed through the few photos and there it was, the girl I had just seen, smiling. On the back of the photo

Bethany Jane 1943

The sun shining in your eyes makes you see things.

But everyone has seen on television the protesters in Middleton Meadow, the girl who appears in every shot holding her childish poster 'Save Bethany's Meadow'. Reporters have not been able to find her, no one knows who she is with and Social Services say they have a duty of care to find her.

Everyone has heard of the strange events when the contractors and police started arriving.

At my house all is quiet, especially at night. Perhaps Aunt Beth never wanted to grow up, I'm sure the sun warms her, provides the energy she needs.

The Exercise

The felt pen scraped across the whiteboard as Gower wrote the last word, RESOURCEFUL, then turned to survey the thirty two people in the classroom. They had readily suggested characteristics that would make a good leader, but did any of them possess those qualities? He smiled to himself, they would soon find out.

Simms looked at the board, this was like being at school; he had been expecting the training to be tough and exciting. He sneered as they picked raffle tickets out of a bucket to randomly select four teams. When they went outside, four helicopters landed; more promising. As each team boarded their helicopter they were blindfolded. The journey was long and silent.

Eventually they landed and were ordered to remove the blindfolds; clambering out, the air felt cold and damp. Blinking in the light they looked around a desolate landscape, they were high up on the moors and there was no sign of the other helicopters. They were each handed a rucksack and warned to duck down, the crew quickly boarded and took off. The eight members of A Team stood dazed; they had been given no orders.

Simms looked around at the others as they took in their surroundings, he decided to act.

'Come on you lot, I estimate several hours till sunset and we need a plan. Everyone carefully unpack their rucksacks and search every pocket, see if we can find a clue to our mission.'

Glad to have a purpose they set to and soon a variety of items and food rations were laid out neatly, every rucksack contained a different selection; pooling their resources was vital.

Someone automatically handed Simms a map, another gave him a small piece of paper. He frowned as he read it, nothing was straight forward; a journey lay ahead but time spent figuring out a plan was essential. They were all strangers; could they make a team, would Simms make a good leader?

He stood up and spoke decisively. 'Each of you tell us your name and briefly what you can offer the team.'

'Dan, mountain climbing and outdoor survival.'

'Felicity, brains.'

'Jane, first aid.'

'Gary, sense of humour…'

As they finished going round, Simms found the words he needed.

'They want us to fail, expect us to fail, I'm sure the other teams will not succeed. Why do they expect us to fail?'

They all had answers.

'I'm female.'

'I went to a posh school.'

'Too skinny.'

Simms spoke out again. 'But we won't fail because we will make a good team, we all have something to offer and we're going to work out our plan right now.'

'So who appointed you leader' sneered Gary.

'I did, no one else took the initiative, but if anyone wants Gary as leader speak up now.'

For a few seconds there was an awkward silence then Dan clapped Simms' shoulder. 'I reckon you're the man for the job.'

The others followed, looking to see what Gary would do.

'Okay man, you win' he said, shaking Simms' hand.

That evening they sat around their first camp fire, tired but positive. Simms and Dan pored over the map; they were on very high ground but had no idea where. Felicity turned out to be very brainy and had decoded the instructions; there was a long way to go yet. Simms stood up and they all looked to him.

'You've done a good job so far, but that was the easy part. It's going to take a long time and the ration packs will not be enough, we must do some more thinking. But first, everyone sit quietly for ten minutes and listen.'

There was complete silence, no distant traffic, no music, no human voices; but it wasn't silent, gradually they tuned in to the sound of running water and the faint bleating of sheep.

'We're in luck, at sunrise tomorrow we'll find the stream, fill our water bottles up and follow it. Those sheep sound familiar, British sheep hopefully, but it doesn't mean we're near civilisation, hill sheep are tougher than humans.'

'Not too tough to eat, hopefully' said Gary.

ooo000ooo

B Team surveyed the bleak hillside in despair as the helicopter disappeared over the horizon. One man upended his rucksack searching for food, a piece of paper fluttered away in the wind.

'What the hell are we supposed to do now?' wailed a young woman.

'You tell us love, I thought you women liked all that equality stuff' grumbled the fat bloke.

'I get low blood sugar level if I don't eat' whined another girl, but nobody was listening as they wandered off aimlessly. The skinny chap sat down on a rock, whichever way he looked there was nothing; delving into his rucksack his spirits lifted, there was plenty of food. If this was supposed to be an initiative test the best thing to do would be to find his way down the hill. In a pocket of the rucksack was a map, he called the others but got no response. Not sure if he was reading it correctly he decided to do a reconnaissance, looking at the map and not at the spongy mounds underfoot, he stumbled map first into a morass.

The fat man and a skinny woman found themselves slithering together down a slope made slippery by tiny rivulets of peat blackened water.

'Wait for me,' cried the girl with low blood sugar 'I haven't got any food in my rucksack, we're supposed to stay together, the others have disappeared already.'

'Don't worry,' said the large man 'it's all a trick, they'll be back to pick us up tomorrow.'

'So shouldn't we stay where we landed?' asked the thin woman.

'No, we need to head downhill and find a sheltered spot for the night.'

'But if it's sheltered they won't see us' whimpered the other female.

Arabella, as she called herself now, sat behind a grassy mound listening to the bleatings of the other members of B Team and of the nearby sheep. Her upbringing as the daughter of generations of hill farmers had long lain hidden beneath her cosmopolitan exterior, but now it would prove vital.

She had thought of herself as a good leader who knew how to delegate, but none of the B Team members seemed capable of any responsibility. She was in possession of a telescope, a Swiss army knife, some food and a strong instinct for self preservation.

As they finished their roast mutton Simms addressed the team. 'We've come a long way in five days, in more ways than one. Once we've crossed that river tomorrow I reckon we'll be near our destination, the drinks are on me tomorrow night.'

After several days Arabella had not seen another human being, let alone B Team, but at last through her telescope she caught a glimpse of figures going in the direction she planned, though too far ahead for any hope of catching up.

The river was fast flowing and Simms was thankful one of the rucksacks had contained coils of rope. It was time to use Dan's climbing skills. Perhaps they had become over confident with the end in sight, but Gary didn't make it across; they were stunned as he plunged in and was dragged under. For the first time Simms made a move that wasn't planned, he dived in. As the cold shocked him he knew he must grab Gary and reach the bank before they were swept away. They both went under several times; in slow motion Simms wondered if they were going to die, they had taken risks on their journey but he had never believed their lives to be in danger. In a last desperate bid he pushed them both to the surface and saw another bobbing head; Dan was in the water but firmly attached to ropes.

They sat shivering and gasping on the banks, when Simms could finally speak he said 'Best team work yet and we've all ended up on the other side.'

Seconds later they were astounded to hear a motor; an old army truck appeared through the trees.

'Congratulations A Team, first back, jump in.'

When Arabella arrived at the river bank on the sixth day she almost gave way to despair, but she had learned, if not a leader, she was at least *RESOURCEFUL*, she laughed the word to herself and imagined how she would tell her story to Gower and the others. The remains of a camp fire, a sheep carcass, muddy foot prints and a rope trailing in the water were proof it had required team work to cross the river; she was too late for the crossing. Resolutely she set off on the long trek downstream to her home village. Her family would be very surprised to see her.

In the back of the truck A Team laughed and joked, imagining hot meals, clean clothes, comfortable beds and a welcoming party. An endless gravel track led to a dilapidated hut for debriefing.

Inside they recognised the figure standing in front of a blackboard. He motioned them to sit on the hard benches; Gary angrily opened his mouth to speak but Simms glared at him.

'Now you can tell us what qualities your leader did have' said Gower crisply.

They obliged, in the hope the debriefing would soon be over.

'Right, now for part two of the exercise.'

The exhausted team members were speechless.

'Simms has been an excellent leader, which is why he is going back out to find the three missing teams. For the rest of you there's a lift back to base for a hot meal and a free bar all evening. Of course, if Simms can persuade you to go with him, fresh supplies are ready... the truck will leave for base in fifteen minutes.'

Outside the hut Gower's assistant nervously approached him. 'There's no sign of the other teams, do you think we should call in the emergency services?'

'No need, we've got a good team in there.' He sighed. 'The lengths we go to looking for a new party leader!'

For Whom The Bell Tolls

He always liked to count the bells; six chimes meant Mummy and Daddy would soon be up, seven chimes and they would be telling the twins to get up for school and at eight chimes the twins would set off for the school bus. He and Freddy were too young to go to school yet, so they helped Mummy and Daddy on the farm. The other helper was Meg the sheep dog; Daddy said she was the hardest worker of all and man's best friend. She was also his best friend, when he was little he thought he was a puppy and sat in her basket.

Today no one was going to school; the church bells were playing tunes, so it must be Sunday. He could see the church up on the hill, but he had never been there. Daddy said Sunday was a day of rest; if you were lucky. Mummy and Daddy were lucky because a long time ago they had escaped from the city; they knew where to go because they followed their dream and found this farm. Then they decided to have some sheep, cows, chickens and children. He liked to hear that story and list the family to himself. Mummy and Daddy had other names to call each other, Ginny darling and Giles dear; the children were Lillian and Rosemary, Frederic and himself the youngest, Percival, named after a knight.

Percival knew he was the favourite, because he was always good; Mummy and Daddy were always saying so.

'Freddy, why can't you eat all your dinner up like Percy.'

'Lilly, Percival is always cheerful in the morning, why can't you be?'

Or 'Percy's got more manners than the three of you put together.'

He was Meg's favourite as well, he slept in the downstairs bedroom as she liked to have her basket beside his bed.

This morning they were all going to the orchard to pick apples, as it was autumn. Under the trees the hens pecked; this was called being 'Free Range'. Mummy took the spare eggs to the farm shop where her friend Abby worked. Percival could count well, he always noticed if any chickens were missing and told Mummy. She told the children they had gone to the farm shop, they must have an orchard there.

When the bell rang twelve times it was lunch time, Percy's favourite part of the day. After lunch Daddy said it was time for a walk.

'Put your Wellingtons on, the track is muddy.'

Percy smiled, he loved going in the mud; that was the only time Mummy and Daddy weren't always pleased with him. Today they all watched Meg herd the white woolly sheep into another field, nobody could run as fast as Meg. Then they helped Daddy bring the four black and white cows in to be milked; they all had names, but the sheep didn't. Percy knew why; the sheep all looked exactly the same and there were lots of them; the cows had their black patches in different shapes and were all girls, Daisy, Poppy, Buttercup and Dandelion. Sometimes Mummy said he loved those girls more than her.

When the bell chimed five times Mummy said 'Let's light the fire as the nights are drawing in.'

Grownups always said strange things like this. When all the children were in bed Percy could hear Mummy and Daddy talking in the kitchen. He was jealous because Meg was allowed to stay up and sit by the fire, just because she was a dog. He tried to work out what they were talking about.

'Ginny darling, you know it has to be done, we'll have to tell the children tomorrow.'

'Oh Giles, I swear that dog knows.'

'We agreed we wouldn't shield them from harsh realities.'

'At least the twins will be at school, but Freddy's going to be dreadfully upset.'

'He's had a wonderful life and at least he's going to the farm shop.'

Percy heard a sort of muffled sniffing from Mummy.

'Anyway darling, they'll soon cheer up when they hear you're going to have another baby.'

In the next couple of days Percy's worst fears were confirmed. The family were all going around looking very sad and Freddy kept crying. How could Mummy and Daddy do that; send Freddy to live at the farm shop and get a new baby instead?

One morning Percival woke up and lost count of the church bells, they just kept ringing, dong, dong, dong, no dings. In the kitchen Mummy and Daddy were cuddling, like they often did and as usual Percy joined in, but this time it made Mummy cry.

'Giles, those bells, why don't they stop?'

'It's old Bert in the village, he's finally pegged it' said Daddy.

'Freddy, are you ready, here's Aunty to pick you up, it will be nice to go and play with Jack, won't it?'

Percival's stomach lurched, they were tricking Freddy, he rushed out to the yard, but Freddy was already being driven off. Meg was sad as well, she was creeping around with her tail between her legs. Percy went back in to finish his breakfast, nobody else had eaten much today.

When he heard a van drive into the yard he hoped Freddy was back, Meg was barking. For the first time ever Daddy was cross with her and chained her up in the barn, still barking furiously.

Daddy was talking to his friend John at the back of the van, Percy went to join in. From inside the van he heard voices that were familiar, but he couldn't understand the words, perhaps John had brought the new baby.

'Come on Percy, you're going for a ride with your friends.'

John opened the van door and Percy looked in. Daddy helped him get inside. The van door closed and Percy called out to Daddy, he had changed his mind, he didn't want to get in. The light from the small windows was just enough for him to see the others. He had a shock, they weren't people; he remembered a picture he had seen and guessed what they were. He looked down at their bare feet and down at his own.

A horrible realisation came over him. His clever mind recalled all those scraps of conversation, his feverish brain did a replay of his life and suddenly he knew. How could he have deceived himself; he wasn't a person at all, he was a pig, just like the ugly creatures staring and grunting nonsense at him. He smelt their fear; did they know where they were going? Percy certainly did.

Four Days In June

Patchwork; a cliché, but the view of Dorset from the car window was of rolling patchwork hills, every shade of green, dotted with darker circles of trees.

Kimberly had not left London since arriving three months ago; replacing the flat ochres and golds of the Western Australian wheat belt with green parks and impossibly busy streets.

She had found Gavin on the internet; they were the same age and shared a great aunt. He was not as she had imagined.

'So you haven't seen the sea yet Kimberly?'

'I didn't bring my bathers.'

'I'm not suggesting we go in, too cold, but the Jurassic coastline is amazing.'

He longed to plunge into the cleansing, chill sea, but he could not let her see the tattoos. She wasn't the suntanned independent Aussie he had pictured; quiet, a girl to ask out, if she wasn't a relative, if his life had been simple.

Tracing family had not been top of the agenda for her working holiday and Kimberly was nervous about this trip to the village where her grandfather was born. Why had she agreed to go with a man she'd never met? He was tanned, hard, but his eyes were kind.

'Gavin, how come you've never met Great Aunty Dot?'

'I've never met my father, let alone his relatives.'

'Sorry.'

'Don't be, Mum's family are lovely, I've got a great step-dad.'

A step-father he was about to hurt.

'What brought you to England, have you got plans?'

'No plans, but I love London; nobody cares who you are or what you were doing back home.' She gazed out at the landscape, so much green in a tiny, overpopulated kingdom. 'Drought in Britain is a dry spring, if they could see our land...'

'Ah... West Bay, our picnic stop.'

They parked by the harbour and looked across at the orange layered cliff.

'Looks easy' said Gavin.

The climb wasn't high, but it was steep, the track had red footholds worn by other feet; one slip and she could roll down swiftly. She stopped to tie her jacket round her waist; clothing in England had continually to be rearranged.

At the top Gavin laid his jacket on a grassy mound near the edge.

Kimberly patted the velvet green in wonder. 'I thought the English seaside would be all flat pebbly beaches.'

As she watched him demolish the picnic, she asked what the plans were.

'I've booked a bed and breakfast for tonight, Aunty's expecting us tomorrow afternoon; then play it by ear. We don't want to put the old girl to any trouble.'

He had a tent in the boot. Honeysuckle Farm, there was sure to be a spare field he could camp in; he would see her safely back on the train to London first.

Kimberly was still crunching an apple when she felt a spot of rain. 'The Sun's rays travel zillions of miles, then one fluffy grey cloud blots them out.'

They clambered down the hill; a heavy shower caught them before they reached the car.

'Charmouth, historic village and gateway to the Jurassic Coast' Kimberly read the sign '…and the sun's come out again.'

Standing on a beach of large pebbles, they viewed the green cliffs that sloped and fell along the coastline. He was enjoying her company, she saw though a fresh pair of eyes.

'The Earth's plates shifted and pushed the land up sideways, that's all I remember from geography.'

She followed him up the grassy slope, past warnings of coastal path closures. They stood on cracked fields that gently descended to the sea, even the diversion had slipped.

'Are you sure we're allowed here?'

The safest ground he'd stood on for months.

'Yes… geography lesson, England is shrinking.'

A muddy wooded path felt safer and they emerged to see the sun sparkling on the waves far below. Her cousin marched on.

'I thought we were stopping here?'

'Let's see what's round the corner.'

'A Lost World' Kimberly marvelled, as they looked down into a dense, green, wooded valley where the cliff had slipped years before. 'If you fell down the cliff, no one would ever know.'

A secret, soft green that would enclose you, spare your family.

'If you jumped off no one would know' he said.

'Gavin, don't be so gloomy, shall I peer over the edge?'

'No!' he felt suddenly giddy and grabbed her.

She was soft and trusting, he should be looking after her; not using her to reassure the old lady when they turned up on her doorstep.

Kimberly was used to flat paddocks stretching endlessly; the drop beneath the grassy edge made her stomach plummet. She was glad to be pulled back, held for a moment. He felt warm and strong, not like a cousin should feel.

Back on the road they drove through dappled green tunnels, trees arching over sunken roads; emerged to sunlit fields dotted with white shorn sheep and chestnut cows.

'Our B&B's the other side of town, historic Lyme Regis.'

She winced as they dove up a steep road and squeezed past a bus. The sun disappeared and they ascended into thick mist.

'Are you sure this is it?'

In answer, the door swung open and a middle aged couple greeted them. '...oh, when you said the lady would like the best room, I thought you were bringing your mother.'

Kimberly's room had a sofa and en suite bathroom. Gavin knocked to see how she was getting on.

'Beats my room at the house share.'

'My attic room is like a house share.'

'You can chill out down here, let's watch television.'

'Okay; seven o'clock we'll go into town and find that fish restaurant.'

He fell asleep on the sofa, it had been an early start. Rain beat on the windows; Kimberly curled up on the bed with extra jumpers.

After dinner she was surprised people were strolling around in the drizzle. Gavin wanted her to see The Cob. Grey waves pounded the stone walls circling the harbour. He held her hand to climb the steps, but the wall, slippery with rain, sloped towards the sea, Kimberly begged to come down.

Along the sea front she admired pink and blue cottages adorned with wrought iron; they found bright yellow houses with green windows and doors.

'Everything is so cute. We must come in the morning and see those galleries.'

In the morning it was still misty; they trekked down a muddy field, dodging cow pats.

'Are you sure this is the short cut to the beach?' asked Kimberly.

Descending through a wood they emerged to blue skies. Children played on the sandy beach sheltered by The Cob and people sat outside their beach huts. The holiday atmosphere made them reluctant to leave.

To him the place was a toy town, full of dolls' houses... but what was real? He wasn't sure any more. She leaned up and kissed his cheek, the lightest of touches, but he felt his eyes prick. Was that how it started, a breakdown, like Mathew?

'Thanks Gav, I'm having a lovely time.'

The kiss surprised her as much as him, did he feel the same way? She couldn't read his expression, he had told her so little about himself.

Aunty Dot's village was perfect; thatched cottages and gardens overflowing with flowers. At 'Honeysuckle Farm' they parked in a muddy lane. A middle aged man opened the door suspiciously.

'Oh sorry, we must have the wrong house.'

'Is that them Brian?' a woman's voice came from inside.

Cautiously he ushered them in. Flowery settees and wooden dressers were nowhere to be seen. Everything was bright and modern, a computer desk tucked into the corner. Aunty Dot was sprightly with rosy cheeks; Kimberly could see the seven year old girl who once skipped through fields.

'Welcome dears, this is Brian our neighbourhood watch co-ordinator and my good friend.'

'I haven't been down here long' said Brian. 'Dot is one of the few originals. I fell in love with the village, now I run my business from home.'

The old lady took down a black and white photo.

'Uncanny, as soon as you walked in the door I saw the likeness; my sister, taken just before she left for Canada to marry her young man. You must have her adventurous spirit.'

'…and Gavin; my nephew was a bad lot, we never knew you existed, Brian was worried you might be an impostor, but you've got the family eyes. My brother would have loved a grandson.'

Gavin felt uncomfortable under Brian's gaze, he must have guessed.

'What are your plans?'

Who was this Brian person? Did he think they'd take advantage of Aunty Dot, she seemed perfectly capable of looking after herself.

'Not sure yet, we're both flexible.'

'Oh you mustn't go yet, we've hardly got to know you' exclaimed Dot 'and you haven't met Amy, they're in Dorchester today, she's having her final check up at the hospital.'

'Oh dear, has she been ill' said Kimberly 'and who is Amy?'

'Another great niece, she and her 'partner' Sam live in a yurt in Brian's field. They're having a homebirth. We haven't had a baby in the village for ages.'

Gavin's plan to camp anonymously in a field seemed doomed. If Brian asked, he was on leave, he still had two days to decide.

'Tell us about your farm Kim dear.'

'East of the Great Southern Highway, we haven't had enough rain for years.' She turned to Brian. 'Granddad married into a farming family.'

'We come from generations of tough country folk' added Dot. 'Our family worked the land, but never owned it, that's why he left. What do you do Gavin?'

'This and that.'

'I feel sorry for young people' said their aunt. 'No job's secure and how anyone affords a house… I admire what Amy and Sam are doing. I was like Gavin, couldn't decide, envied the older ones who had been away during the war.'

'What did you do?'

'Stayed here, started working for the local doctor, then his son… I wanted to buy a retirement flat in Bridport, but I can't sell this cottage; when buyers do a survey they run a mile, it's made of branches and mud.'

Brian took them to the window and pointed up the hill, a roof glistened in the sun.

'Solar panels; barn conversion, everything ecologically friendly; plenty of room if you want to stay a few nights. Amy and Sam stayed all winter, the yurt lost its appeal in the snow.'

Kimberly hesitated; if she stayed they would want to know more.

'We mustn't keep you Brian' said Dot, as they finished afternoon tea.

Only the chocolate box village and the delicious cake fitted Kimberly's picture of how this day would be.

'Dear Brian knows how to take a hint; one advantage of being old is saying what you like. Now what brings you two lost souls here? Only known each other two days, but you seem close, kissing cousins, nothing wrong with that.'

Kimberly blushed. 'I'm not adventurous; they packed me off to get away. Mum and Dad are on the point of walking off the farm, the land's worthless without rain, our neighbour committed suicide. Generations of farmers and all that's left is me and hundreds of acres of dust. Granddad didn't want you to know.'

'...and do you think that would be the worst thing that's ever happened to him?' She looked directly at Gavin. 'Kimberly's uncle was killed in Vietnam.'

She knew. He felt cold to the core; to break down in front of a girl and an old lady would be unbearable. Was this what it was like for Mathew? Invincible when they were over there, but back home...

'You didn't get a tan like that in England, why the secrecy, you should be proud' said the old lady.

'My step father is very proud, especially the medal; he won't be when he knows I've gone AWOL.'

Four Days In June was published in Dorset Voices by Roving Press 2012

70

Garden Visitors

Since last century probes have been going out, heading beyond our solar system, taking messages into the unknown, sending radio signals of their progress back to Earth. And on Planet Earth we keep listening, giant dishes constantly turning, alert for any radio signal from afar, any message from another planet, another solar system; any reply to the pulsating signals we have been radiating out for decades.

And I nearly trod on the Alien Life we have wondered about for centuries; nearly consigned our visitors to the compost heap. Digging and weeding ready for the summer bedding, watched by the robin, stooping motionless so he would be brave enough to pick out a grub, I spotted a glint. Long buried broken glass or a lost jewel? I wiped the mud off on my gardening trousers, held it up to sparkle in the sun and nearly dropped it with the sudden burst of heat.

Placing it on the kitchen windowsill I washed my hands and contemplated; pretty enough to hang on a chain around my neck, an historic find? No, this was not an ornament that had lain in the cold ground for centuries, already it was scorching the paint work. With the kitchen tongs I put it into a cake tin, then took a picture on my mobile phone; it was too precious to share on Facebook, instead I sent the picture to Uncle Gerald.

My initial excitement was replaced by fear, was it radioactive? As I willed my uncle to reply, I noticed the tiniest of movements. I rummaged in drawers for a magnifying glass, darting back every few seconds, loath to let the jewel out of sight.

My mobile vibrated just as I positioned the spy glass, a multi faceted surface, but every facet was moving.

'Uncle Gerald? How soon can you get here?'

Uncle Gerald was not a scientist, he was a photographer mad about macro; cute fluffy yellow bees to alien insects with grotesque eyes, the tinier the creature the more fascinated he was. Infinity goes outwards and inwards he used to tell me when I was a child.

Now, as he adjusted his eight inch long lens, I continued to peer through my inferior glass. The sparkling facets made it difficult to see, but something was emerging.

'Can you see anything yet, looks like this ornament has been colonised by tiny ants.'

He put down the heavy camera and rubbed his eyes.

'How lucky you put it in the cake tin, to think they could have been lost. I always told you to be observant in the garden, but I didn't expect you to come up trumps like this.'

He adjusted his lens while I peered through the magnifying glass again. The facets were all open and tiny dots were still coming out.

'Can you make out what they are?'

'They certainly aren't ants, but I need to think before we get too excited.'

'Are you going to take a photo?'

'I don't want the flash to go off, they've already had a shock, but the lighting isn't right.'

'Do ants or dust mites, whatever they are, get shock... and surely there's enough light coming from the bauble?'

'The patch in the garden, when was the last time you dug it over?'

'Autumn, when I put the spring bulbs in, but this thing's so small it could have been there without me noticing.'

'If it has been there all winter it must be self heating... when's Stephen back?'

I had never seen such a strange look on my Uncle's face.

'Not till next week.'

'...and nobody else knows about this, that dreadful woman next door's not likely to pop in is she?'

'She's at work and I'm not expecting any visitors, I wanted to get on with the garden, the weather being so nice on my day off.'

He lowered his voice. 'We'd better whisper, imagine how loud we sound to them.'

I laughed. 'Billions of insects co exist with human noise, funny, I've never asked you if they have ears.'

But Gerald wasn't listening, he stooped motionless over the cake tin, hardly breathing, there was a smooth click.

'Do you want to look?'

'No, I'm useless with your super lens, everything swims before my eyes.'

He took a few more shots. 'Have you locked the back door? We need to look at these on your computer screen.'

As he headed for the kitchen door I glanced down to see the bauble rotating gently.

Through the magnifier the black creatures were increasing in numbers, swarming in an orderly fashion, fanning out to the edge of the round cake tin, reforming in shapes like a horizontal murmuration of starlings.

I beckoned Gerald back and we watched, fascinated as the tiny black dots circled the bauble then strung out like a neat spider's web.

'They can't be ants, they're not trying to climb out.'

'In which case it's safe to leave them for a few moments.' He handed me the memory card out of his camera. 'You get the pictures up on screen while I set up the ICCTV.' He looked at my puzzled expression. 'Insect closed circuit television.'

I looked at the screen, then crept back into the kitchen. 'What else have you got on here; some of your weird friends from camera club?'

'Of course not, I put a brand new memory card in before I left home, first rule of photography. Go and look again, objectively.'

It could have been a flash mob dance shared on U-tube, filmed from a distance; they were still small, too small to see the expressions on their faces, or to work out exactly what they were wearing, but I was looking at a crowd of people. Uncle Gerald was not the sort to play practical jokes, so who was playing a joke on us?

'They're disorientated, panicking' he said, as I returned once again to the kitchen table.

'I'm not surprised, who wouldn't be, stuck in a giant cake tin, the burnt on bits of cake must look like rocks to them. Tell me this is all a dream.'

'The only fact we know is it is not a dream. Come on, what are your theories?'

'That bauble emitted some sort of invisible drug vapour, if we go and look at the screen again, we will just see ants.'

'Cameras can't hallucinate, no theory you come up with can be stranger than what we are seeing.'

'A secret space station shrank as it plummeted back to earth?'

'A lot of people and it is like no space station yet built.'

'No, because it has come from the future and shrank as it travelled back through time.'

He frowned.

'Well you come up with a better theory.'

'I was thinking they must be aliens, I don't know why we assume aliens must be human like and why they are always portrayed as being our size.'

'So they came from a tiny version of earth?'

'Their planet does not have to be smaller. Earth has supported dinosaurs, blue whales and insects.

'But such a tiny vessel coming billions of light years through space?'

'Our space vehicles are tiny compared to space.'

'What are we going to do? Mum was looking forward to hearing the patter of tiny feet, but not that tiny…'

I could feel a bubble of hysteria, but Uncle Gerald was obviously going to take this whole thing seriously and logically or was he?

'Actually, I have no idea. Is their little vessel still well stocked with food, have they a good leadership structure. Are we keeping them prisoner or protecting them?'

'Is this their first venture into space or have there been many, lost in the ocean, lost in the garden, or even washed down the drain. Who shall we tell?'

Suddenly he grinned. 'At last I have something to contribute to the society.'

'You mean the Royal Photographic Society?'

'No, no, mere amateurs. What I am about to reluctantly tell you must never be spoken of. OHMSS... Order of Her Majesty's Secret Scientists. Mark from Uni. got me in as official photographer. Only the Prime Minister knows of its existence, one of the confidential things the Queen chats about at her weekly audience with the PM. We deal with anything it's not wise to let the public know about.'

'Sounds like something out of Doctor Who.'

'Yes, there was a big who ha, we wondered how on earth the script writers found out, luckily the public didn't believe it. Expect an invitation to Downing Street or Buckingham Palace, you'll have to be sworn in.'

'Me, I don't know about science things, this is so bizarre.'

'You have to be sworn to secrecy.'

'If this society is real, have you dealt with aliens before?'

'I'm only in the lower ranks, hardly been called upon yet. But I'm honour bound and privileged to report to them immediately.'

ooo000ooo

And so I received an invitation I could not refuse, it was Downing Street, I was not important enough for The Palace. But I was left in no doubt that I had taken a solemn vow of secrecy. So that is why no one must ever read this document.

Holiday

'Where's the sea Daddy?' said Casie, as we stood outside Bournemouth Railway Station.

Our long journey south had been tiring and tedious, but I had kept my young daughter's spirits up with the promise of a seaside holiday. Now all we could see was a bus station. There was no sign of a welcome or promise of summer fun as the rain that had splattered the train windows now fell in a deluge. I could not afford a taxi, nor did I wish to draw attention to our arrival and presence in the town. In my anorak pocket was a Christmas card address for my Aunty Linda and a map printed off the internet.

She was not expecting us, had probably given up hope years ago of my mother or anyone in our branch of the family coming to England to visit her. I remembered her as an unorthodox live wire who dumped her boring husband to go to Bournemouth and paint.

'I'm hungry, you said we could have fish and chips at the seaside.'

I had promised Casie a few things in her short life, let her down, but this time I had to keep the promise I had made silently. We were wet and hungry, but at least she was safe.

We passed a large Asda, I resisted the temptation to go in for emergency supplies to pacify Casie. I also wanted to avoid CCTVs.

All we could see were tall buildings and traffic, my hastily printed map did not include the station, the only landmark on it was Bournemouth Pier. Even if we found the address there was no guarantee Linda still lived there.

A group of students giggled as they passed us, stepping in puddles, no coats or umbrellas, speaking in French or Spanish.

'Which way to the sea?'

It was a simple question with a simple answer; they pointed straight across the busy road then to the subway. One of them offered Casie a small bar of chocolate and helped her unwrap it. We made our way through a passage, a couple of scruffy old chaps sat leaning against the wall drinking, but took no notice of us. So far we had met no one who would care what we were doing. Up on the roads lined with shops and offices I gave Casie a piggy back, the chocolate boost to her morale had worn off; it seemed a long way, but when large hotels loomed in sight, I knew we were heading in the right direction.

The cliff top was windy and wild, but I was childishly excited to see the sea. I pointed out the pier to Casie; it was shrouded in misty rain and she was not impressed. But I had found my marker; the train journey had been long enough for me to memorise the route to Aunty Linda's house, the map would have disintegrated if I had taken it out in the rain. If she still lived there she should be in; late in the afternoon in this weather any normal person would be at home cooking dinner. For a second I wondered what was happening in Glasgow. Lena was expecting me to bring Casie back any moment now. I picked her up this morning, didn't see him, he was still asleep.

We back tracked past the hotel, turned left, more hotels, but there it was, the only house in this part of the road; long front garden, flowers beaten by the rain, a green front door. My heart was thumping.

The door was opened by a middle aged woman with flowing skirts and wild grey hair, she did look familiar, but it had been such a long time.

'Aunty Linda?'

'Kevin?'

'No, it's me, Callum.'

'I would not recognise either of you, I thought with the little girl…'

'Kevin's got three now.'

'This is never the baby your mother said you were expecting?'

'Yes, meet Casie, Casie say hello to your Aunty Linda.'

'Come in, come in, the others will have a surprise.'

'I have a lot to explain.'

'Don't explain anything yet, dinner's nearly ready… Natalia, are you downstairs?... she's got a little girl, dry clothes are what we need, we've probably got something to fit you in the collection for the shelter… in here…'

My daughter was stunned into silence and I let the activity wash around me. Other people had appeared out of various doors, more than one language was being spoken, towels were produced, Linda showed me a downstairs toilet just in time for Casie.

We sat at a long table in the kitchen. Linda at one end, Slava, an older man introduced as her partner, at the other. On either side were a variety of people, some frankly weird, perhaps vulnerable would be the right word, sandwiched in between were several children.

'This is my great niece Casie, don't you just love her accent.'

'She hasn't spoken yet' laughed Slava.

Later, Aunty Linda took me up to her studio, the only room out of bounds to everyone.

'Don't worry about Casie, Natalia's very good with the bairns and her daughter seems to have taken a shine to your wee one.'

With my daughter being tucked safely into bed it was time for me to explain, but Linda hadn't finished speaking.

'I used to hope your parents would send you and Kevin down here for a holiday, not having any of my own. I fantasised about bucket and spades on the beach. Now my friends are always busy with their grandchildren and I haven't got any of those either. So I'm going to make the most of having wee Casie around, let's hope it'll be sunny tomorrow.'

'Thank you for everything, this is an amazing place, goodness knows what we'd have done if you had moved or weren't in, but you may not want us to stay, I'm in a terrible mess.'

'Your mother didn't say your marriage had broken up.'

'We weren't married, not really living together, so there wasn't a lot to break up. Poor Mum felt like she never got to do the grannie thing, though she has

Kevin. At least he didn't let Mum and Dad down, house, wife, good job, brilliant children.'

'Never mind about him, have you got custody?'

'I haven't got anything. Me and Lena were engaged, she lived with her Mum, I was still at home, I didn't think about future problems, we were just playing mummies and daddies. She met this bloke, more exciting than me I guess, but then I discovered he'd hit her. I asked around, he'd got previous, his own son was in care. Suddenly I had to act like a grown up, I didn't know what to do. Lena thought I was trying to interfere. I tried to get proper help, but she wouldn't co-operate. You hear about these men; 'Where was the real father?' If I wait for all that official stuff it could be too late. When Lena understands why I'm doing this we can make a fresh start.'

'If only it were that simple Callum, Lena must be frantic, but you're right, no one will listen to you, so no one must know Casie is here.'

'Do you believe me?'

'Do be honest Callum, I don't know… I don't know you, but if what you're saying is true we have to think very carefully before we let anyone know you're here and you certainly can't go anywhere else tonight…'

She was interrupted by the shrill doorbell and frantic knocking, her words became urgent.

'How likely is it your mother would guess where you are and tell the police?' She paused, for a moment there was silence in the house. 'Sounds like Slava's opened the door.'

The silence didn't last, we heard heavy footsteps on the stairs.

'Just stay here with the door closed... if they come in, let me do the talking.'

I could not hear what was going on, minutes seemed to go by, then the door swung open and two uniformed officers marched in, one male one female. Had Casie and I been betrayed, by my mother... or Aunty Linda, she'd had plenty of time to call them herself.

'I'm sorry Callum.'

My aunt looked shocked rather than guilty. The female officer asked to be taken to see my daughter. The policeman took off his hat.

'Are you Mr. Callum James Cambell McCready?'

I hardly recognised my full name until he recited my address.

'Yes, but please let me explain...'

'I'm sorry sir, I have some bad news for you, it's about your er... your daughter's mother.'

I was slow to understand who he was talking about in his English accent. Without his hat on he looked as young as me and nearly as nervous.

'There's been an incident involving Miss Lena Anne Leyman at her home...'

It was my Lena he was talking about, he recited her address, he stuttered out more words.

'...I have to tell you she is dead.'

My mind was now clear. 'Did he do it? Why didn't she listen to me?'

'I'm sorry sir, I don't know anything about the case, it could have been an accident, but the police in Glasgow need to speak to you.'

At that moment Aunty Linda burst back into the room.

'Callum, I'm so sorry, thank God you brought poor wee Casie away. You'll have to be strong for her, she can stay with us till your mother can get down.'

'What do you mean?'

'Don't you understand, you'll have to go back to Glasgow to clear your name.'

'But surely nobody thinks…?'

Invisible

I always joked I was invisible, but actually being invisible turned out to be far worse than being treated as invisible.

I referred to it as the White Hart Syndrome. We had been for a walk in the country park, put our muddy boots and the dogs back into the car, then strolled down to the village for lunch. The White Hart was the only place open for refreshments in winter, but had an appetising menu and we selected what we wanted. Then my husband realised he had left his wallet in the car, despite warning signs at the car park

Do Not Leave Valuables In Your Vehicle

I had to go to the bar to order. We had a joint account, I didn't mind using my debit card, but we weren't locals and I was a woman, would they notice me?

It was quiet, a few people eating, a few drinking. Behind the bar someone was bent double loading the glass washer, a young man was replenishing the award winning crisps, a grumpy woman my age was demonstrating to a young girl how to wipe down surfaces and a person of indeterminate sex was chatting on their mobile. I sidled along, hoping to get the best vantage point to catch someone's eye. No luck. I cleared my throat. I scanned the bar for any notices I might have missed. Were we too early or too late for food? Was there a bell I was supposed to ring? I heard a couple at a table nearby comment in amusement that there were five people behind the bar. My stomach rumbled with hunger. I turned to glare at my husband, but tucked in a cosy nook, he wasn't looking my way. A hot flush came over me and I struggled to take off my chunky knit jumper.

I contemplated yelling 'Fire!' to get attention.

The hot flush persisted, I needed to get outside. I marched back to our table.

'We're going' I hissed, grabbing my coat.

'To another table?'

'No, out.'

Confused husband followed me. We had to pass the bar to get out, a head suddenly popped up.

'Can I help you?'

'Too late… we've got a banana and a bottle of water in the car we can share' I added pathetically.

You probably think I'm paranoid, but I have always been invisible. First day in upper sixth, Jenny Woods said to me 'Whose class were you in last year?'

'Yours' I replied with gritted teeth.

Last month I went in that newsagents' with the post office. I was buying several newspapers for my neighbour. Just as I got to the counter the man darted off to help the post office woman, a whole two feet away. I expected him to look up, perhaps utter a few words *Sorry, be with you in a moment.*

I helpfully fanned out the papers so he would see how many to be scanned, but his back was turned, her head was bowed. I was invisible.

I crossed over the road to the Co-op, hoping the newsagent would be puzzled to find the papers arrayed on his counter. At least I didn't steal them; I was tempted, but didn't want to end up as a fuzzy picture on the front of the Gazette

Police Seek Shoplifter

'This magazine's free with The Sun' said the Co-op chap.

'No thanks, The Sun is not for me,' I hastened to add 'it's for my neighbour.'

'They might like the magazine.'

'Okay, yes please' I smiled.

It was good to be visible and have a conversation.

I felt guilty keeping the magazine, but looking back, I probably saved old Mrs. Carson next door. It was new, hence the give away; a magazine for intelligent readers that didn't stereotype on grounds of age or sex. It was also celebrity free. There were interesting articles, the middle pages were devoted to intriguing puzzles; it was too good to pass on to Mrs. Carson.

Later that evening I started reading about the work of a psychologist who wanted a cross section of society for his research on assertiveness, or lack of it. Travel costs and a week's free stay in a country manor, what wasn't to like?

'Sounds a load of rubbish' said my husband.

'No, Professor Bleivinis is not running a course, he is a firm believer that people should feel comfortable in their own skin, not try to change; nobody is going to get thinner or become successful.'

'A week away while the 'Tour de France' is on, hmm, pity it's not three weeks.'

'So you don't mind if I go?'

'Not at all.'

I went on line to find out more and before I knew it an hour had passed and I was pressing Submit.

We were a motley crew of twenty, the only passengers getting off the train at Berryford Halt. A small coach awaited us on the patch of gravel that passed for a car park. Wherever we were going it was certainly secluded.

The first few days were great fun, rather like being selected for Bletchley Park, but without the pressure of having to save your country. We happily submitted to health checks which would have cost a fortune on Bupa and been unavailable on the NHS. Good food, a wonderful spa and swimming pool, walks in the glorious grounds and most of all, intelligent conversations with interesting people. The tests were a more elaborate version of the ones we had completed on line; from clever puzzles to probing questions about our views on life. Somehow nothing felt too intrusive in the relaxed atmosphere.

Ten of us were accepted for the second week. I was proud and my husband delighted when I phoned with the news. We were allowed one call each on the landline.

But has he told you what it's all for?

I hardly had time to answer my husband's query before my three minutes was up.

'Research… of some sort, I'm just glad to know my mind and body are in such tip top condition.'

You are probably wondering what Professor Bleivinis was like. Not how you imagine a professor, an insignificant little man you would not notice in a busy street.

Tuesday of week two was when everything changed. Five of us were summoned to the library, we seated ourselves at the antique desks.

'Congratulations on being selected for the Real research' he said, in his usual quiet tones. 'Forget HG Wells and Harry Potter, the in depth bio-cellular tests reveal you are the perfect subjects. I trust you are all feeling well?'

'Never better,' said Something-in-the-City Simon 'who wouldn't be after such a healthy holiday getting away from the family?'

'The radioisotopes you took in your breakfast health drink are due to start working in one minute. On the piece of paper in front of you write your reactions as you experience them.'

I guessed this was part of the psychological tests, he hadn't really given us anything. But as I started writing...

I am feeling a tingling all over as if I had just had...

Better not write that, I mused and looked around to see what the others were doing. For a moment I thought I must have been in a trance and the other four people had undressed, slipped out of the room and left their clothes draped over the desks. But the sleeves were moving, a jumper bounced up. I closed my eyes and shook my head. When I opened them my pen was writing by itself.

I am having an hallucination, so vivid I can feel the pen in my hand...

I lifted my hand and the pen floated in the air. The sleeves of my jumper were too long, I rolled them up, I felt the tight cuffs round my elbow, but my arm was not there.

You have given us a psychotropic drug, or whatever you call it, I refuse to believe what is happening to me.

'Good, good, keep writing…'

I looked up to see a smile on the professor's face I had never seen before.

I stumbled to my feet, the clothes were walking around, solid. I tottered over to the elegant Victorian mirror. I was a vampire, I had no reflection.

For a moment there was stunned silence in the old library then urgent cries.

'Yes,' said the professor 'you are all invisible.'

'No, it's some psychedelic trip' croaked the Tshirt and jeans that belonged to the teenage boy.

'All done with mirrors' the denim shirt sleeves of Sally the firewoman drew circles in the air.

'Prove it to yourselves by undressing,' said Professor Bleivinis 'no need for modesty.'

'This isn't right,' the jacket of Something in-the-City Simon shrugged aggressively 'you had no legal right to do this.'

'You all signed the consent forms, you are all highly intelligent people capable of reading the small print, you were free to walk away like the others did.'

'Will it wear off?' I could feel the tremor in my voice.

'I don't know, I haven't seen my staff for weeks.'

Suddenly it all seemed so obvious. We had never seen any staff; the whole place was kept immaculately clean and meals ready precisely on time. The staff weren't efficient and discrete, they were invisible and presumably nimble, naked and silent. Perhaps the other volunteers had escaped, we didn't see them go.

'I'm out of here' said the checked shirt darting towards the door. 'I'm going to prove this is just a trick to test our reactions, I've got a friend who knows that illusionist on TV.'

'If you think that, you're free to go,' said the professor 'but you'll find it is wiser to stay, you will all need counselling; going out into the world will not be easy unless you intend to dress yourself in a burqa.'

The door slammed and checked shirt had disappeared. Suddenly laughter filled the room and the denim sleeves folded themselves across the large denim bust.

'I'm a feminist, you really expect me to turn up for work at the fire station in a burqa?'

'You could claim your right to respect at work' I could hear the hysteria rising in my voice.

Suddenly the professor's arm was moving up and down. The T-shirt was shaking.

'This is amazing, we'll be famous, thank you professor. I can't wait to get back to Sixth Form and the girls' changing room...'

Professor Bleivinis stepped back and shrugged the invisible teenager off.

'This is a serious scientific experiment, not a joke, we could help national security.'

'Of course it's not a game' I cried 'how can we go home?'

I was cringing in a corner, I had taken my clothes off and it was true. My watch floated in front of me, I could not see even my little toe, only the floor. At that moment the door burst open and a pair of boxer shorts entered.

'It's true, I put my boxers back on in case we suddenly become visible again. This place is full of invisible people, we bumped into each other.'

The boxer shorts moved towards the professor. 'What are you going to do with us now, we need answers or we go to the press.'

If the professor had been able to see the man perhaps he would have dodged out of the way. We saw his chin tilt up, he stumbled back, his heel caught on the hearth of the old stone fire place. There was surprisingly little blood, but Sally, with her first aid experience, confirmed he was dead. We had all seen how hard his head had struck the stone mantle.

'Bloody idiot,' said Simon, his shirt sleeves waving above the boxer shorts, trying to find some purchase 'what have you done?'

'I just wanted some answers' said boxer shorts.

'Well we won't get any now, will we?'

Jane

'Jane will not be joining us this evening.'

The guests looked up in surprise as Professor William Montecute entered alone though the double doors. The occasion was the annual charity dinner that William and Jane always hosted. An event more important for the prestige of attending than whichever charity was being supported.

The professor turned to usher in a stunning young couple. 'Jane has been called away to New York on urgent business, but I leave you in the capable hands of Annabelle and Rupert.'

The guests gasped at how like her mother Annabelle had become. Her twin brother Rupert had also inherited his mother's high cheek bones and dancing eyes, but there was no mistaking the strong jaw line of his father now he was no longer a boy. They had the poise and confidence that came from being head girl and boy at their progressive boarding school. They each took a side of the long gallery and went to greet all their guests with royal dignity. With all the attention on his children only the closest of associates would have noticed William's mask slip to reveal an air of distraction.

Not many guests remembered or cared which charity their one thousand pound tickets were helping; it was always something medical involving children or women in third world countries. Last year it had been for reconstructive surgery best not discussed over the five course meal.

With the absence of the ever vigilant Jane some of the women flirted with William as they filed into the elegant dining room. If their husbands noticed, they were safe in the knowledge that their wives could never compare to the beautiful Jane. As the twins had not yet passed twenty it was assumed Jane had not yet passed forty.

The dinner was excellent as usual.

'Who are we eating tonight,' laughed a guest 'Percival or Persephone?'

'Boris or Betty probably,' answered William with equanimity 'the rumours about the wild boar getting onto the estate were well founded. Persephone and Priscilla have produced the most delicious suckling pigs, wild boar crossed with the best Montecute Suffolk.'

The guests savoured the roast pork with relish. The estate farm shop was renowned for miles around and the lovingly restored wood stove in the Tudor kitchen added an extra dimension of flavour. Not for the Montacute Suffolks the acres of mud and mini air raid shelters that were the lot of most outdoor reared pigs, they were free to roam the ancient woodlands on the vast Montacute lands.

'...and how are the residents of the walled garden?' asked Doctor Graham Fellows.

'Never better...'

Doctor Fellows always enjoyed the meal, but was far more interested in Professor Montecute's scientific work, which involved anything from providing pigs' heart valves to the NHS to testing Kevlar body armour for the Ministry of Defence.

'Just like their country cousins their lives are happy and stress free till the day of their demise.'

Other guests were not afraid to ask questions, that was part of the evening's entertainment.

'I do find it a little creepy, William dear, that none of us knows what goes on inside the medical unit.'

'You do know, because I am always happy to tell you. No one minds our pigs being humanely killed so we can eat them, an evening's enjoyment. So why bridle at pigs being killed so someone can have a life saving operation? No one is allowed in there except my assistants, because we cannot risk infection.'

'But is it not all still vivisection under a different name' asked Annabelle provocatively from across the table.

Sometimes William wondered if the progressive school had engendered too much independent thinking.

'Not at all, you should be proud that we are the most advanced medical establishment in the country. Why, the pigs in the body armour experiments receive better treatment than soldiers in the field, in fact the soldiers in the battlefield receive excellent treatment because of our research.'

'But the soldiers choose to join up, the pigs don't' she retorted.

William was still unfazed. 'The only pigs with a choice are those wild boars that the locals are so worried about, at least our animals are not condemned to a life of factory farming.'

The other guests nodded in agreement, but Annabelle had not finished.

'Doesn't your research help rich celebrities with their cosmetic surgery?'

'If the rich want to pay for their vanities and insecurities, that's up to them. They're overcharged, the money filters through to those who need it and the surgeons get the practice they need to reconstruct genuine victims of accidents and burns.'

'Quite so,' said Doctor Fellows 'my field, as many of you know and may we ask how the other branch of research is doing?'

'Certainly, to put it in lay terms for the rest of you, we are trying to move away from surgery, or speeding up results after surgery by encouraging self healing. You look at a new born baby with its perfect skin, if a baby needs an operation his body heals quicker than an adult's. On the farm open days you all love to see the piglets, they are pink and smooth like human babies, their skin is velvet, so like us and yet so different, you cannot help but be fascinated. We study genes and hormones to find what it is that enhances healing, makes cells reproduce themselves.'

The professor combined intelligence, compassion and charm, nobody ever won an argument.

Rupert took his role as host seriously and suggested it was time the next course was served. By tradition the arrival of the sweet meant lighter chat.

'How long will your mother be in New York?' Someone changed the subject.

'No idea,' said Rupert 'we only just broke up for the holidays, been busy studying for our A levels, we don't take much notice of what's going on at home.'

It was his children's absence that had enabled William to keep to himself the fact that Jane had not gone to New York. When the guests had finally left, the three of them stood on the grand steps.

'A wonderful evening, you were both splendid, thank you so much, now I expect you both want to get upstairs and check your emails and Facebook or whatever. Do you have plans for the holidays?' he added hopefully.

'Yeah, we'll let you know at breakfast' said Annabelle.

'Don't expect me down till lunchtime,' added Rupert 'I think we deserve a lie in.'

'Goodnight Daddy,' his daughter kissed his cheek 'I bet you want to go and have a nice private chat with Mummy, still early evening in New York.'

William slipped through the now silent house to Jane's room, the twins' suite of rooms was out of sight and sound at the top of the house.

'Hello Darling, how are you feeling? It all went splendidly, everyone said how much like you Annabelle is.'

'How I was' muttered his wife, sniffing.

Jane never liked anyone to see her when she was not at her best. Her glamorous international beauty business was successful enough for her to leave most of the travel to others and country life with William was what she loved, in contrast to the shallow world of commerce. She attributed her clear skin and youthful looks mostly to her healthy lifestyle. She was over forty, but no one would have guessed. It was very unusual for her to feel ill, but now she did, she agreed with her husband that quiet rest in a dimly lit room, with herbal remedies, was best.

'But I do wish you would let me have a mirror.'

'Darling, you know how much you hate seeing yourself without makeup, you would only feel miserable if you saw your red nose and puffy eyes.'

'I must look awful, thank goodness this room is so dark.'

'You don't look awful to me' he lied.

'Could it be an allergy?'

'No, no, it's flu, did you manage to eat your supper?'

'I didn't really feel hungry, I couldn't face the meat, I just ate a few vegetables.'

'Try and get some sleep.'

She patted the bed beside her. 'I'm not used to sleeping alone, let's cuddle for a moment.'

'Sorry, I can't risk catching germs and giving them to the pigs, you know that.'

He hovered by the door to make it look as if he was reluctant to leave.

Professor Montacute did not go straight up to the marital bedroom on the first floor, but to his laboratory. Jane was deteriorating at an alarming rate and it could not be long before she noticed something was seriously wrong. He could not turn to his colleagues for help, even to Graham Fellows. He was not a cold hearted scientist, he loved Jane and knew he should never have let her talk him into trying the new treatment. She was beautiful as she was and did not need enhancing or preserving, but her beauty had given her a vanity, her career and position as lady of the manor had made her feel she had an image that must be preserved. He checked the results on the blood samples he had taken from her earlier. The results were irrefutable and he was no nearer finding a solution.

He went to bed in the hope that fresh ideas would come in the morning, but sleep was impossible. When the bedside phone rang it startled him, it could only be Jane using the internal line.

'William, please come now, I feel awful, something's the matter with my hands.'

He raced down the sweeping staircase, down the narrow butler's stairs into the wine cellars, then down the winding tunnels that dated back to Cromwell's time. He unlocked Jane's door.

She was sitting bolt upright in bed. 'I've got some awful disease haven't I, or is it cancer? My hands are swollen and they feel so stiff. I won't have to go to hospital will I?'

'Of course not Darling, I can do every medical test here, in the meantime some strong anti-inflammatories should help.'

Recoiling inside, he hugged her reassuringly.

'Rupert and Annabelle, they still think I'm in New York?'

'Yes, you know what teenagers are like, more interested in their own lives.'

'Good, I don't want to worry them, spoil the Easter holidays.' She tried to smile 'My face feels stiff now.'

He clasped her hands before she could touch her face. 'Take the sleeping tablets, you'll feel better after a sleep.'

After a fitful few hours William went down early to the kitchen before the staff came in to clear up after last night, before his son and daughter were awake. He made up a breakfast tray.

His stomach lurched when he saw the empty bed, but then he heard the shower going and hoped it was the sound of the water that made Jane's voice sound muffled. He went in holding a towel in one hand and feeling the water with the other, it was cold.

'Her words were slurred, he could only just make them out.

'I was so hot...'

He helped her out, but she stumbled and for the first time looked down at her feet. For a moment he saw terror in her cloudy eyes then she became agitated.

'I need to get outside, let me get fresh air, it's spring, I want to walk in the woods, smell the earth.'

'Don't be silly Jane, it's still chilly outside and you don't want the staff to see you.'

His eyes began to brim with tears as he saw her eyes water; the sapphire eyes that he had first noticed at university were faded grey.

'Let me tuck you in with the breakfast tray and we'll go for a walk later if you're feeling better. I'm just going to get some more medication.'

William Montecute fled to his laboratory, locked himself in and wept. For the first time since boarding school he was not in control of his life, or was he? The most appalling idea occurred to him and yet it was the kindest thing he could do, an act of love. But not yet, not while there was still hope. Once again he started on his furtive route to Jane's room, he could hear Annabelle in the kitchen chatting to the staff.

As he ran down the corridor he could hear her terrible cries, though it didn't sound like Jane at all. He hesitated to open the door, but when he did he was pushed roughly out of the way, knocked off his feet. Jane did not know her way around the labyrinth of tunnels, but she was heading in the direction of the only exit to the outside, the old ice house secluded in the woods.

With the rapid thinking and logic of a scientist he curbed the urge to run after her, he must get to the woods before she emerged, but first he rushed to the room where the research weapons were kept. In moments he was skirting round the stable yard. If Jane was still feeling ill at least she would be moving slowly.

The old wooden door to the ice house was locked, she must still be inside. The woods were mercifully quiet, sudden loud squealing told him she had reached the other side of the door. Even as he paused for breath and considered his next action, the door began to splinter, there wasn't time to think. He blasted away with the high velocity rifle until the door collapsed inwards to reveal the bloody remains of a dead sow.

The logical side of his brain told him he had made the right decision, instinctively he looked around, certain the noise would have drawn some of the staff to see what had happened. Then he heard twigs crackle and out of the trees emerged several Montecute Suffolks sniffing the air. They were docile, used to humans wandering in the woods, but he couldn't be sure; they had never scented blood before. In their cosseted life death and violence were unknown, but as William pointed the gun at them they sensed danger and retreated.

He had to keep a clear head, his first instinct was to shoot himself, but even if there was enough ammunition left that was the coward's way out, the least he could do for Jane was to be around for the twins. If Jane was reported missing, it would not be long before it was realised she had never got on a plane. But there would be no body found, no evidence of a crime, only the results of the latest M.O.D. experiment.

After a difficult struggle with the stretcher trolley the pig was in the dissecting laboratory and William's blood stained clothes were put in the medical incinerator along with the experimental serum.

**Jane was first published on
Cutalongstory.com**

Lost

It started with a plastic clip, one of those gadgets you didn't know you needed, till your mother ordered them from one of those catalogues full of things you didn't know you needed...

Now I couldn't find it to seal up the bag inside the cornflakes packet. Hardly a major drama, but odd, because the drawers in our brand new house were still so tidy I knew where everything was.

But that was the least of my worries on Day One, Monday, first day of my new job, first day without Seb. My husband had left for the airport and his new job yesterday; he would be travelling to many places, but working from home in between; hence the buying of a house on an up market estate in a northern market town, where prices were so much lower than London. At last we had a foot on the property ladder, but two weeks in Nigeria scared me almost as much as if he had been a soldier going to Afghanistan.

The estate was lovely, in a surreal sort of way, no two houses alike, not a single road was straight. Mothers could push prams and children ride bikes along traffic free lanes; if they could find them amongst the swathes of newly planted trees. Seb and I had strolled the scenic route to the shiny toy town shopping square, located the bus stop for the frequent purple and white buses into town. My new job was in a smart office near the trendy café in the square, it should have been easy to get to work.

I locked the royal blue door of number 7, Mill Pond Road. Our two storey white house, with matching blue shutters, I thought of as French. Next door was a Cotswold stone bungalow, while the other side was a tall, narrow, red brick town house.

Across the road it was New England pale blue timbering and as I walked to the corner I passed a flint cottage and the Spanish stucco. Ten minutes later I realised my amused musings on the architecture had distracted me from the route; I turned down a footpath only to be confronted by a high brick wall. I could not see over it, but knew from the roar of the traffic that this was the 'feature wall' that originally surrounded the grounds of the old Victorian asylum. It had been retained to separate Woodbury Village from the busy A road lined with 1930s semi-detached villas. I was far from Saint Anne's square.

'You must be lost' called a young woman, edging backwards out of a red front door with a push chair. 'I'm always redirecting new residents.'

'Thank goodness I'm not the only one, I don't want to be late for work.'

She led the way expertly. 'I've got to pop into the estate office, we're still within the guarantee period and there's something wrong with the plumbing. Make sure you inspect your house for any possible faults, even a cupboard door that sticks, they're obliged to fix it.'

'Did you have Dianna Denby as your agent?'

'Her of the orange makeup, dyed black hair and too high heels?'

I giggled 'She keeps calling and ringing to ask if we've settled in okay.'

'As if she had generously donated the house, not signed us up to a huge mortgage, can't stand the woman. I'm hoping it's her day off, that young bloke is usually very helpful.'

My day passed quietly, too quietly, I worked by myself and at lunch time the only person I spoke to, as I rummaged in a basket of sale curtains outside 'Homestyle Fabrics', was the dreaded Dianna.

'Oh, hello Mrs. Strickland... they would go delightfully in the kitchen, probably only need taking up an inch... has your husband gone overseas yet?'

I didn't recall telling her, Seb must have let it slip. She already acted as if she shared the home with us, I didn't want her sharing my life as well.

'Soon' I lied.

'No problems with the house?'

'It's perfect thank you.'

Lilac Lane, Mulberry Crescent, Hawthorn Way; I followed the route I had jotted down from the map in the office, hoping that would work better than recognising the scenery. Winding roads, curving cul-de-sacs, I saw my house sooner than I expected, but as I approached, something was wrong. It was sandwiched between a miniature yellow castle and a Georgian villa. The houses in Woodbury Village were not all the same, but they were not all different; I read the road sign, Oak Crescent, the number on the identical blue door was 4.

When I finally arrived back at Mill Pond Lane I greeted my house with relief, but as I let myself in there was a cold emptiness. I picked up the mail, mostly New Home cards and went to the kitchen, half hoping that Seb had magically reappeared to put the kettle on. There was something missing from the little kitchen table.

I was sure I had left the note with a phone number on, the number of Seb's colleague who lived in the town; his wife had said I must ring so she could pop round to introduce herself. I felt irrationally upset that I might have lost my first local contact.

The phone rang, it was my mother.

'Yes of course I'm fine, Seb's only been gone one day. No of course I don't mind if you and Dad don't come up till Liz's baby's born.'

Last week it had seemed helpful we were to be left in peace while mum fussed over my sister, now I felt a tinge of envy imagining Liz surrounded by loving family. The last straw was when I couldn't find the scissors to cut open the carton of chopped tomatoes. I just wanted to make a quick pasta sauce and I was certain the scissors were in the drawer. I took out the tin opener and made do with baked beans on toast.

I kept myself busy that evening, half watching mindless soaps while I hemmed up the bright curtains; of course Dianna Denby had been right, she probably knew all the window measurements on the estate by heart and they did make the kitchen look homely.

I was woken before the alarm by the sound of car engines, no wonder I hadn't seen any neighbours if they went out so early. It was bin day; as I wheeled ours round through the little side gate I noticed the blue pot of daffodils was no longer by the front door. They were there the evening before, a house warming present from Seb's mother; they were light enough for anyone to carry away, but who would be mean enough to take them?

Seb's long email that evening was an entertaining description of his arrival and I tried to think of a cheerful, newsy reply. As I pondered, the phone rang, it was an older woman's voice.

'I'm Linda, I know my husband was supposed to pass on our number to Seb, I expect he forgot. I know what it's like being in a new place. That's how I got into the home parties thing. It's not Anne Summers; home furnishings, no obligation to buy, but my next one is on your estate, it would be an ideal chance for you to get to know your neighbours. Next Tuesday, number four, Oak Crescent, tell them I invited you.'

I suddenly started laughing, relieved to have someone to chat to and told her about the identical houses. 'I just hope I can find it again.'

'Tell you what dear, I'll pick you up on my way there, I can introduce you properly.'

The outing was fixed, I wasn't sure if I would enjoy it, but I could reassure Seb I was settling in.

My light hearted mood did not last as I went into the kitchen; my favourite fridge magnet, a souvenir of our first holiday together, had vanished. I knelt on the floor, assuming it had fallen down, but all I found was the shopping list it had held in place.

Wednesday passed pleasantly at the office. I checked my emails on my smart phone and Seb said he would Skype at the weekend. I was used to working in a busy place and I coped easily with my new work.

But when I returned to the house I had a feeling as soon as I walked in the door that it was not my home. I had no rational explanation and told myself it was Seb's absence.

I resolved to buy items to stamp my personality on the house when I went to Linda's party. I walked into the lounge to close the curtains against the dusk and immediately saw it was gone, the crazy colourful cushion my sister had made me for my first bed-sit. I shivered, how could a whole cushion disappear when no one had been in the house? Nothing else was disturbed, no signs of a break in. I timidly inspected the rest of the house; all was as I had left it.

The evening was endless. I sat miserably in the kitchen with reheated leftovers from our Sunday roast, a meal that mocked the cosy lunch with wine I had enjoyed with Seb. I went to bed early, looking nervously out of the window at the quiet street.

On Thursday morning I double checked the windows were locked, left the curtains half closed, tidied every room, pushed the front door twice to make sure it was locked.

At lunchtime I browsed in the card shop for possible baby cards and chatted to the girl behind the desk. I went in the greengrocers and bought healthy vegetables for a stir fry. At the post office I scanned the notice board for things to join, but I knew none of the locations, let alone how to find my way home again in the dark. The main advantage of the tiny flat we had rented in London was its close proximity to the tube station and bus stops; I suddenly felt isolated.

The house was as I had left it, note pad on the phone table, magazines in the same place on the coffee table. I put the radio on in the kitchen, hummed to the music; but when I reached in the drawer for my usual knife to slice up the vegetables, it wasn't there.

I yanked the drawer open, my small collection of kitchen tools lay neatly in the tray, but no knife. I had used it at breakfast to cut fruit, washed and put everything away before I went out.

That evening I sat with my phone as company, but my mother did not want to talk for more than a minute, worried she would miss a call from my sister, who was enjoying a last meal out with husband and friends. When I did catch a friend at home I let her do the talking, reluctant to tell her about my strange week.

On Friday evening I walked home automatically, I had more to worry about now than getting lost; with good reason. As I crept into the lounge I saw straight away that the picture was missing from the wall above the artificial fireplace. It had not fallen down, it had disappeared. Seb called it his family heirloom, his grandmother had wanted him to have it. Painted by her grandfather, it was not a masterpiece, of no value to anyone else, but we both liked the rural scene.

I sat in a daze with my mobile in my hand. I could hardly dial 999, but what was the number of the local police station? A burglary with no sign of a break in, did other houses on the estate have identical keys? I dialled 999. I tried to sound intelligent, not hysterical; rational but scared; after all, the thief could be hiding upstairs.

'Yes of course you did the right thing calling us, but the house is secure, no sign of a break in… we haven't had any similar incidents on the estate. Keep your phone by your bedside, if you hear anything during the night dial 999, don't investigate it yourself.'

When Seb skyped on Sunday I didn't tell him, he would only worry. After all, I had come to no harm. I told him about work, my visit to the town on Saturday, library, art gallery… I did not tell him that the wedding present vase in the hall was missing from its nook when I got back, nor about my visit to the new lady vicar earlier. Who else could I talk to about my fears that a brand new house could be haunted?

On Monday evening the vicar came round to visit.

'I could pray for lost souls, after all, who knows what dark suffering there was at the asylum,' she looked at me and smiled reassuringly 'but I'm sure it is more likely that someone has kept duplicate keys for the new houses.'

When I went in the kitchen to make her a cup of coffee, the flowery bone china mug was missing from the cupboard.

'You must visit the police office in the square, it's only open on Tuesday mornings, the officer is very nice, don't be fobbed off.'

P.C. Sutcliff was very nice, though I doubted he believed me.

'Now Mrs. Strickland, let's go through the obvious things first. How many doors do you have?'

'Front and back, no patio doors, if that's what you're thinking.'

He laughed 'You would be surprised how many people forget to lock them. Okay, how many sets of keys?'

'Two, my husband's keys are hidden at the back of my bedside drawer, they haven't moved.'

We then went through dates and items missing, on paper it looked pathetic.

'Now I have to ask some questions which are personal, please don't be offended. Have you ever suffered from depression, stress?'

'Not until I moved here.'

'Good, good… have you ever been unfortunate enough to have a stalker, or is there anyone you could possibly think of who has a grudge against you or your husband?'

'No, no we're just ordinary people.'

'There was no particular reason for moving up here away from friends and family?'

'Do you know much it costs to buy a house in London? Sorry, sorry… I expect you get all sorts of weirdoes… I mean people with mental health issues, wasting police time.'

He laughed 'You said it, not me. But this appears to be a genuine burglary incident so we will investigate. I shall ask around and I or another officer will call with advice on security, though it sounds as if you are doing all the right things.'

I nearly jumped out of my skin when the door bell rang at seven o'clock that evening, even though I was expecting Linda at exactly seven o'clock. It was the first time I had heard the door bell since we tried it out on our arrival.

As I helped Linda carry her boxes up to the door of Number Four, Oak Crescent, the security light came on revealing a blue pot of daffodils by the doorstep. If my face showed surprise, the large box in my arms hid my expression from the other woman. The garden centre was probably full of pots the same. I could hardly accuse our hostess of theft.

The second surprise came when the door was opened by Dianna Denby; she looked equally shocked, but quickly regained her composure during the introductions.

'You will feel at home here Mrs. Strickland,' she trilled 'all the houses on the estate have magnolia walls and oatmeal carpet.'

It wasn't just the walls and carpet that were identical, in the hall was my vase in the same nook, but perhaps it was coincidence, our gift had no doubt been bought at TK Max or Homebase. But when I caught a glimpse through to the kitchen and saw my curtains it was hard to stay rational. Dianna could have suggested I buy them because she knew how good they looked in her own kitchen. But considering she took such an interest in our home, why had she never mentioned she lived in its twin?

All rational thought left me when we were shown into the lounge. The identical beige sofas could mean she also liked Ikea, but not the presence of my unique cushion. My flowery mug was on the same coffee table and I looked up to see Seb's painting hanging over the fireplace.

Lost was first published in An Eclectic Mix Volume One   by AudioArcadia 2015

Macro

Ben was crouched down motionless, Claire stood silently a few feet away, her bag heavy on her shoulder, the sun beating down on her face. In the bag was their picnic, beach towels, sun tan lotion, the newspaper and her paperback.

Ben stood up and peered at the screen of his camera. 'Bother, bad shot and he's gone now… no wait, there's a green one… hold the camera a moment while I get the other lens out.'

Claire nearly collapsed under the weight; she wondered if they would ever make it down to the promenade. At that moment another photographer appeared, his chest criss-crossed with straps, black cases swaying against his hips as he made his way down the steep zig-zag path.

'Good spot here, south east facing wall, found any yet?'

'Seen some, but no good shots.'

Ben assessed the newcomer. 'Ah ha, Nikon, you've got the D4 I see, how do you find it?'

'Brilliant, just trying out the 105 F2.8 lens.'

'Looks like his is bigger than yours' said Claire, as the two men compared their macro lens.

'I've spotted four different species here' the man turned to her, in the mistaken belief that she was interested.

'I've only seen green ones and brown ones. How can you tell, when they're so small?'

'Experience. They're territorial.' He pointed to the stone wall with its pattern of cracks and holes.

'Is that why they have numbers painted above each entrance' she giggled.

Ben frowned at her. This was not the way to address a man who was obviously a professional photographer and naturalist.

'Do you mind if I carry on Ben, I need to catch the sea breeze and cool off.'

'My wife's not interested in lizards' he apologised.

'Handy to have someone to carry your sandwiches though.'

Ben knelt back down and peered through the view finder, but the other photographer was hogging the best position. He was about to give up when he saw it. Claire was right about the sun being too hot, probably just a mark, but the magnifying lens was showing him a number forty two painted in bright red, above the hole where stones converged.

Magnified, the eroded gaps looked like cave entrances. He lowered the camera; he could see nothing with his naked eye. The other man was crouching, totally absorbed. Ben cleaned his lens then let the camera roam steadily over a small area; number seventy three in blue, fifty seven in yellow… one of those artists who writes the bible on a grain of rice, an installation artist in miniature?

The title of tomorrow night's camera club competition was 'Close Up' and Ben had still not taken a picture he was satisfied with. At that moment something darted out of fifty seven… not a lizard. He zoomed in closer and an angry face glared up at him. Ben nearly toppled back on his haunches.

Several tiny faces, their expressions readable; they had a green tint to their complexions and a blue hue to their frizzy hair, but they were human faces. When wings opened and they darted upwards Ben realised with relief they were insects and tilted his camera upwards. He felt a tiny prick on his hand and then another, but he was more aware of the cramp in his knees as he tried to hold the camera steady. Rare insects were not to be missed.

He suddenly felt light headed, more tiny people were emerging from a larger opening, above which, written stylishly in green, were the letters HQ. They were all carrying… no, his eyes must be tired. He set his camera to continuous shoot, struggled to his feet and leaned against the wall. The other man was bending over his camera case.

'I need a cold drink, time I joined the missus.'

'Okay' the other photographer nodded vaguely in his direction.

'No more pictures?' Claire was surprised to see Ben packing away his equipment. 'Are you alright, you're looking a bit odd.'

'It's too hot, let's have a swim before our picnic.'

'Umm, it's ages since we went swimming together.'

'Not together, we'll have to take it in turns to look after the camera.'

That evening Ben downloaded the pictures onto his computer, it could be an advantage that Clare was not interested, he needed to check every single shot before any one else saw them. On to the large screen came a picture of a green lizard, its beautiful patterns could only be appreciated in this way. There were plenty of pictures of the wall, lizards darted away so quickly… next were the insects, but he had never seen insects that looked like this… insects didn't wear clothes for a start.

He trembled as he scanned through dozens of pictures; all the creatures were standing on two legs, their arms in waving positions and their bodies clad in diaphanous garments of beautiful hues. Their features were sharp, their rosebud lips caught in a variety of expressions. The next shots showed their wings open, arms clasped to their chests and legs pointed neatly like ballet dancers. Then the final few pictures; he had not imagined it, they were carrying bows and arrows, not the string and stick toys of children, but intricately carved wood with strings of shiny silk, spun by a spider perhaps.

He shook himself, pushed his chair back and stood up; he was beginning to believe it was real. He stooped to peer at the last picture; two creatures were pointing at a yellow poster, he jumped when there was a knock on the door.

'Ben, come and look at the local news, it's that man we met today.'

He met her at the door before she could see the screen and followed her downstairs.

'No, not this bit, it will be on in a moment.'

They sat through a traffic accident, the resignation of a football manager, a sea rescue, then Claire nudged him.

A local conservationist has spoken of his shock at the underhand behaviour of the local council. By chance he spotted a small planning notice at a site of special scientific interest.

They saw the photographer talking in front of the familiar wall.

Of course these cliffs have long been subjected to man made interference and nature has adapted, but we need to preserve what is left, the cliffs are home to rare lizards, migrating sand martens...

...and fairies. The words came unbidden into Ben's mind.

A local councillor started speaking.

We need more amenities to bring holidaymakers and to make our wonderful beaches accessible to the disabled.

'No, they can't put it there' exclaimed Ben.

'You and your lizards,' laughed Claire 'there's plenty of cliff left for them.'

'Umm... I'll just get my pictures ready to email off for the competition.'

Upstairs Ben closed the study door and sat down at the computer. He examined each picture, zoomed in closer and soon built up an image of the fairy village. How he longed to have one of those tiny medical cameras; to penetrate the little creatures' homes would be amazing.

But there was plenty to look at on the face of the wall; a lizard with a fine silver chain around his neck and a lead attached, the picture with the yellow poster. He could read it now and so could the fairies; it was the planning notice, no wonder they were angry. There was one more picture. A splendid looking fairy, the leader perhaps, was holding a large piece of cardboard, as if he was hitch hiking, but the boldly printed words read HELP US.

Ben closed down the computer, he needed to think. Who could he tell? Who should he tell? Claire, the press, the environmentalist? No one would believe him unless they saw the pictures... he made a decision, then vowed to put everything to the back of his mind at work the next day.

Ben did not have to seek out the expert. At the camera club meeting the man they had met at the cliff was the judge for the competition. Everyone's digital images were in the club computer, ready to be projected onto the large screen that had been used for colour slides in the pre digital era. It was too late for Ben to change his mind, the hard plastic chairs felt even more uncomfortable than usual.

The pictures were of a high standard; bumble bees with fur soft enough to stroke, flowers barely noticed in the field, but beautiful close up, emerald and indigo dragon flies and a spider eating its prey. Some pictures were very different, a spiky forest revealed as human skin... then came Ben's first picture.

Lips open in surprise the little person stood outside number seven, hands on hips. There was a burst of laughter, but the pictures were anonymous, only the winners' names would be revealed at the end.

The judge looked bemused or annoyed, it was hard to tell, but he quickly pulled himself together.

'Well I recognise the home of a rare lizard, the wall under threat from the council, nice sharp picture, someone's obviously done a lot of work in Photoshop.'

The next picture was Ben's favourite, two fairies holding hands, skipping. He had not worked out if they came in two sexes, presumably they reproduced, but to him they looked androgynous.

The judge was perplexed. 'Do the rules allow for digital manipulation?'

He moved swiftly on to the next picture, Ben's last; more laughter, though not from the judge. It was the fairy leader holding up his HELP US placard and beside him stood a bold looking fellow, his bow and arrow pointing at the planning notice.

The bumble bee won and a flower came second. No one had guessed Ben was responsible for the fairies and he joined in the amusement.

But in the car park the judge sidled up to Ben and handed him a USB stick and his card.

'I thought I was going mad, but it seems I'm not the only one who's seen them. Ring me. We must save the cliff, but publicity would be a worse threat to the fairies than the cliff lift. By the way, your picture was best.'

Maestro

The man stared at the large white screen and mouthed letters to himself; B B C R A D I O L I V E... none of them seemed to form any recognisable German words. He climbed several steps up onto the stage and peered behind the screen; there was a chair and a small bureau, on this was a strange metal object and a neat pile of paper. Much neater than his bureau, but who would bring their work to a concert hall? He peered at the sheets, but the writing was tiny, not in his own language, nor French, perhaps English. The stage was empty of players, but there were more chairs than he expected, he looked around, impressed with the large auditorium. He heard footsteps and expected to see his friend appear, then realised with delight it was a long time since he had heard footsteps on a wooden stage. His head felt clear, the buzzing gone. But it was not Franz the inventor who appeared, but a tall gaunt man in strange clothes.

Simon Simmons, the Radio Three presenter, looked forward to the rest of the day. He had enjoyed a pleasant lunch and he was on time for the afternoon rehearsal. Another town, another concert hall, another orchestra and a conductor he had never met before; Ukrainian, Polish or Scandinavian? It didn't matter; one of those brilliant young polymaths who spoke several European languages perfectly and had studied in all the major cities.

The music was well known to Simon, he had his notes ready for the seven thirty p.m. live broadcast; all he had to remember was the conductor's name and how to pronounce it.

The conductor looked older, shorter than he expected and if he dressed that flamboyantly for a rehearsal, the audience could look forward to a colourful concert. He was checking the music on the stands, a punctual and efficient man thought Simon as he approached him with arm outstretched.

But the conductor did not shake his hand, instead he peered arrogantly at him and spoke volubly in German. Perhaps he had forgotten what country he was in, not surprising the way these maestros charged around the globe.

'Welcome to England.'

The conductor ignored him and stepped up onto the rostrum to examine the music. They both turned to the sound of approaching footsteps. A young man in jeans and T-shirt appeared from backstage, he spoke in perfect English with a precise East European accent.

'Good afternoon, you are from the BBC? I am glad you could come to the rehearsal.' He lowered his voice. 'Is that your sound man on my rostrum?'

'No, I thought he was the...' Simon did not want to offend the world famous conductor. 'He's not with us, so he is obviously not meant to be here, though he does look familiar, shall I call someone...'

Before he could finish they were interrupted by the sharp guttural tones of the stranger. The conductor looked puzzled, but replied in German and approached him. The two engaged in lively conversation, but Simon worried about the stranger's body language and hoped the situation would not turn into an incident.

The conductor patted the man's arm and turned to Simon.

'I presume he can't understand English, I think he's German, but I can't grasp his accent. We may have a, how do you say, 'nutter' on our hands, he thinks he is Beethoven.'

Simon felt a lurch in his stomach, that's where he had seen the man before, in paintings; no, too much wine for lunch. He should fetch the building manager, the stranger was not their responsibility.

The conductor laughed. 'He does look like him.'

The stranger scowled, well aware they were laughing at him.

Simon had an idea, it seemed a shame not to harvest the situation for future broadcast anecdotes, especially if they let him do The Proms this year. He motioned to the Steinway piano relegated at the side of the stage, not needed for this evening's concert.

The conductor smiled in agreement. 'Let Beethoven prove by playing to us.' He turned and spoke in German to the stranger, who strode over to the piano, then halted. He examined the instrument, lifted the lid carefully and propped it open, then fingered the keys as if they were a lover's body. He played a few chords, held his ears, then nodded in approval.

As he played exquisitely, both men recognised a Beethoven sonata, though the tempo was faster than they expected and he added extra flourishes.

'So he's a brilliant musician,' said Simon 'as are many visiting soloists. Ask him what today's date is.'

A few brief words were exchanged.

'Twenty Seventh of February'

'That's today's date.'

'1813...'

'...Okay, so he's a Beethoven expert, he would know the right dates, Seventh Symphony composed...'

No one was listening to Simon; the two men were absorbed in German conversation, as if the young conductor was enjoying a private masterclass. The stranger turned back to the keyboard tenderly trilling the high notes then suddenly hammering chords.

The conductor stood up straight, his eyes shining like a teenager in love. 'He IS Beethoven, no one could make up what he is telling me.'

Simon groaned inwardly, two insane men on the stage and the orchestra would arrive any moment.

'What are you saying, that he's a ghost?'

The conductor put a protective arm round the stranger and placed a hand on Simon's shoulder. 'He's as solid as you or I, as alive, more so perhaps; a time slip? I cannot explain, but we must protect him from the truth. Ludwig says he went to visit his inventor friend Franz, who claimed to have a machine that would help his deafness, then promised a visit to a new concert hall to see if it had worked. Let him enjoy his time with us, he could be whisked away at any moment.' He looked anxiously towards the back of the stage as they heard voices. 'You must look after him while I'm rehearsing, if he strays outside the building onto the busy main road the shock would be too much.'

'Of course, he could be knocked down by a car, never get to write The Ninth.'

Simon could not believe he was going along with this ridiculous melodrama, but it was too late to discuss it further.

There was a murmur as the conductor introduced a former teacher and mentor, then a flurry of tuning and movement of chairs.

'Let's start at the beginning of the third movement, put more life into it than we had yesterday.'

The conductor drew breath and the orchestra launched into the third movement of Beethoven's Seventh Symphony.

Simon closed his eyes in delight, the concert hall acoustics were perfect for this orchestra, but they had only played a few bars when the stranger leaped up from Simon's side, uttered guttural words of disgust and clamped his hands over his ears.

The orchestra were astonished when he strode up to the rostrum and even more astonished when he seized the baton and the conductor retreated. It seemed several players were German or spoke the language, they frowned at the accent, but soon grasped what he wanted and pointed to the pages of music to help their colleagues. Several times Beethoven raised his arms and halted them, stepped down, threaded his way to the back of the orchestra, tapped shoulders, pointed at the music, then returned to the rostrum before the conductor could reclaim it.

At last he tapped the music stand, turned the sheets and everyone understood they were going to play the whole work.

'What shall we do?' whispered Simon urgently to the awe struck conductor.

'Nothing, there's only room for one Maestro in this town.'

'But this evening's concert?'

'If he's still here he must conduct.'

'But your picture's in the programme and what shall I tell the Radio Three listeners?'

'They can't see him, tell them what you like.'

The orchestra played with such vivacity Simon feared they could never repeat such a performance for the real concert. When it was over everyone sat stunned, then the conductor rushed up to hug Beethoven, who didn't look too pleased.

'Well done everybody,' said the conductor 'go and have your tea and relax.'

Beethoven spoke rapidly to him and the conductor turned back to Simon.

'Okay, we have to leave the stage, I think he's saying words to the effect it's time for a beer, but first he needs to go out to the courtyard for a slash. I'll guide him to the gents and keep him away from the outside doors, you go up to the cafeteria and order the three of us the best meal they can rustle up.'

Simon looked at his watch. 'I have to link up with 'In Tune' give them a preview of tonight's concert...'

But the two men were gone and the sound engineer had arrived to check Simon's microphone.

Making an Entrance

His name was on the billboard in larger letters than mine.

'Live Satellite Broadcast from the National Theatre.'

They had that wrong for a start, this run down theatre in a godforsaken seaside town could not afford live broadcasts; the locals would see a recording at a Sunday matinee tomorrow.

While Charles was making his entrance at the National Theatre tonight, in front of a packed house, with cameras sending high definition digital images around the world, I would be making my entrance on the splintered stage of 'The Regal'. Ticket sales had been poor, considering there was nothing else to do here on a Saturday night.

Charles and I had started out in rep. together, touring provincial theatres. Now I was back touring those same theatres, looking a lot the worse for wear, as did the theatres.

The posters for 'Murder in the Tunnel' showed my co star Sylvia in her television days; it seemed unlikely anyone would remember that dreadful series, but judging by the age of the audiences so far this week they probably would. Sylvia had had so many face lifts she wore the same surprised expression throughout the play, it was left for me to portray shock, guilt and grief. The other three members of the cast performed multiple costume changes to come on as uniformed police, detectives, lord and lady of the manor, gardener, postman, railway guard etcetera.

Charles was a national treasure, the National Theatre play had been written as a vehicle for him by one of the Alans; the other members of the cast were also great thespians, some on their way up, others on their way down.

I had resisted reading about the drama, but it was impossible to ignore, discussed on Radio 4, Radio 3, BBC Four, BBC Two and in the broadsheets. Charles' character looked back on a long life with a mixture of emotions, but in the final act he was moved to commit suicide, not out of desperation or melancholy, but for altruistic reasons. It was a complex story that raised issues, but provided no answers.

Our little play was a revival of a cliché ridden black comedy drama that any simpleton could understand. One of many similar dramas I had acted in over the decades. It was one of those long forgotten plays that I had been in many years ago that gave me the idea. I could not remember what it was called; Perfect Murder... Perfect Alibi... Quiet Death? But our landlady's daughter had said I made a perfect murderer, though it was the chap playing the policeman that she slept with.

Was that before or after I married Gillian? Can't remember now; Gillian would have been a national treasure by now and I was the first to admit she had a greater career ahead than I could anticipate. We weren't one of those couples where the wife steps back and supports her husband. I encouraged her to take every opportunity; she did and ran off with Charles.

Years later, when it was fashionable, he came out as gay, making the stealing of my wife an even crueller blow. A few years further on, when that was fashionable, he came out as bi-sexual, which I supposed helped explain.

Of course I couldn't have made my plans without the internet, you don't need to be a scientist or doctor to find out about drugs and chemistry. Nor could I have acted without my intimate knowledge of the backstage area of the National Theatre, acquired in happier days.

A mini cab to the nearest town with a railway station, fast train to Waterloo and fast train back again in time for the evening performance and my mission was complete. In the final act of Charles' play he retires to his study, pours his whisky nightcap into the crystal tumbler, drops something in and sips it like a connoisseur. Being Charles, he likes the real thing, no cold tea for him. He had his favourite single malt and knew the exact level on the bottle, woe betide any stage hand who took a secret swig.

Amusing that he would play a character wiling to part with his life; Charles clung tenaciously to his life and career. He didn't cling to Gillian, dumped her for the next girl, or perhaps it was a boy. I offered to take her back, no pleaded, but she refused, said we couldn't turn the clock back. Maybe it wouldn't have worked with us, but nor did her new life, things went downhill after that, what with the drinking. No one remembers her now.

I made my entrance that night feeling an extra buzz, even most of the audience stayed awake. I was on stage in every act, a perfect alibi. The audience laughed, mostly in the right places and as the curtain came down those who weren't afraid of exertion applauded. We had given the locals a good evening out.

'Are you coming to the matinee tomorrow?' asked Sylvia, as we left through the stage door.

'I didn't bother to buy a ticket.'

'Oh dear, they've probably sold out, Cousin Daphne bought our tickets weeks ago.'

Sylvia had been saved the ordeal of the B&B when her spinster cousin invited her to stay in her tiny two bedroom bungalow, thrilled to impress her neighbours with her link to fame.

I doubted the matinee would take place if my plan had worked and wondered how soon it would be on the news. In the pokey attic room with no sea views I switched on the small television hunched under the sloping ceiling. Football, grand prix, the middle east, politics, then as tomorrow morning's newspapers were previewed, the rolling words beneath.

Theatre legend dies on stage.

For a moment I fantasised that he had forgotten his lines, that would have been almost as satisfying... then the presenter spoke.

We are just receiving news of the death of one of Britain's greatest actors. A fellow cast member said he died as he would have wished, in harness. It is believed he passed away of natural causes while feigning death in the final scene of the award winning play by Alan...

Now for tomorrow's weather.

I waited irritably for the next round of new items.

...of the audience were surprised when he did not appear for the curtain call, but other members of the cast smiled as a man in a suit explained that Charles was feeling a little under the weather after being on the stage for three hours...

...viewers in cinemas and theatres across the world saw his final moments. When stage crew could not arouse him, paramedics were called. A spokesman for Saint Thomas' Hospital said an elderly man had been admitted with a suspected heart attack, but was declared dead soon afterwards.

If only Charles had been alive to hear himself called an elderly man. Natural causes a bit disappointing, though I guessed that would count as a perfect crime; of course there was bound to be a post mortem.

The morning news was much the same, but I switched the set off when the accolades and anecdotes started rolling across the screen. My not so 'Full English Breakfast' was interrupted by the arrival of Sylvia and Daphne. The cousin looked distraught, while Sylvia wore her usual expression.

'We had to come,' said Sylvia 'what terrible news, weren't you in rep. with him?'

'He was my favourite actor,' sobbed Daphne 'I've followed his whole career, I saw him at Chichester.'

'They won't show the matinee now,' said Sylvia 'but we shall still go to the theatre this afternoon, take some flowers to show our respect.'

When I strolled round the town later that morning there was a sign outside 'The Regal'. Friends and relatives of Charles had requested the showing go ahead as a tribute. I popped into the ticket office and spoke to the ancient volunteer behind the desk. She didn't recognise me.

'You're in luck, we've had a few returns for this afternoon, one broken hip and two deaths.'

I rang Sylvia. 'Yes, row D43 and44 and E46, bit of luck. Allow me to take you two ladies out to tea afterwards to celeb… remember Charles.'

To celebrate indeed, to watch the perfect crime unfold on the big screen.

Making An Entrance was first published in Kishboo e-magazine in 2015

MoonLighting

'Only one towel Sir,' said Emma politely 'may I see your membership card?... I know you're a regular, but I still have to swipe your card.'

We exchanged exasperated glances as I trudged past with a trolley full of wet towels.

'Have they got those lockers fixed yet?' asked an irate lady, as I struggled down the stairs with a pile of folded clean towels.

'Sorry, I keep asking the manager.'

'At least the showers will be clean if you two girls are on duty.'

I smiled in agreement. Emma and I worked harder then the boys, though we had little thanks from the manager. We were all receptionists and life guards, but we also had to clean the toilets. Emma was saving up for university and I couldn't find a better job. Emma was pretty, even in the faded yellow T-shirt and grey jogging bottoms that passed for a uniform at 'Excelsior Health and Leisure'. When dressed for a night out she was stunningly beautiful.

Emma had the occasional date with members, but also came out with our group; the boys may have been lazy, but they were also good looking and great company. Other friends tagged along, we were all free, single, poor and most of us lived at home; it was a good crowd.

At first we didn't notice when Emma didn't join us, but soon it seemed she hardly ever came out with us and we gossiped.

She's probably got posher friends than us.

Maybe she's met someone.

Why not introduce him?

Understandable, new boyfriend, you don't want to show him off till you know he's secured.

Or there's some reason why she's too embarrassed to show him.

Married man, older, ugly?

At work Emma was bored and restless.

'Stick it out Emma,' I said 'it's only for a short while, then you'll be going places while I'm still waiting for my aquarobics teaching course to come up.'

'I want to be independent, have enough money not to worry when I start university.'

'How can you be? This job barely pays the rent on your grotty room, but at university you can live in those halls and get a student loan.' I looked over her shoulder at the local paper, flats to rent. 'That's a dream.'

'Maybe not, I've been doing some evening work.'

'Oh, so you haven't got a secret boyfriend.'

'No' she said sharply.

'Where are you working, Piza Express, Macdonalds?'

'No thanks, this place is bad enough, it's a private company.'

'Office work, courier?'

'Personal assistant.'

'Good for you, using your brains, that's got to be more interesting than pushing a mop bucket.'

The next evening Mum and I went to the pictures, one of those films Dad didn't want to see; the arty cinema in town, not the multiplex. As we left we almost bumped into Emma coming out of that posh restaurant next door; with her was a very smart man, older than her but fit.

'Hello Emma, Mum and I've just been to see that film, it's really good.'

I paused, waiting for her to introduce him, but at that moment an elegant car drew up and he opened the back door for her. With a little wave she slipped in, he closed the door and walked round to the other side; she didn't even have to slide across the seat.

'Who was that?' said Mum.

'Emma from work.'

'Hmmm he was rather nice, bit older than her.'

'He was yummy, no wonder she's been so mysterious lately. A bit young for you Mum.'

'Just because I'm on a diet, doesn't mean I can't look at the menu.'

At work I asked Emma.

'Oh, he's one of the company clients, in town overnight.'

'Was the food nice at that place?'

'Divine.'

For some reason I didn't mention to the gang that I had seen Emma. Work trundled on as usual and she took the odd day off sick, that was not unusual at the Excelsior, but when Emma was off for a few days in a row and I hadn't heard from her, I was worried. Her mobile was stuck on messages, my emails remained unanswered, so on early shift I went round to her house share.

'Emma? She left a week ago I think, no idea where she went.'

She had never said much about her family and when I called the others we realised none of us had her home address or contact number.

After worrying that night, I was surprised and irritated to see her at work the next morning.

'I kept trying to ring you Emma, Mum says if you're ever not well you can come and stay at our place.'

'I was fine, busy moving.'

'You managed to get a flat?'

'Yeah, the company helped me.'

'Shall I come and see... where is it?'

'I can't tell you... security reasons.'

Perhaps you will think I was naïve, but I thought a good company would look after their staff and want them to live where it was safe to take company lap tops home. A few times I asked Emma if she was coming out with us and she would reply 'maybe next time.'

Occasionally I noticed her giving out business cards to gold card members, the blokes who could afford Gary or Phoebe as their personal trainers. Her company must have been pleased she was promoting business locally.

One day on early shift Emma said 'Let's go to that new café after work, the one that does everything in chocolate.'

I readily agreed, glad she was still up for girly outings.

'I wanted you to be the first to know' she said, as I dipped a sticky doughnut finger into luxury hot chocolate.

I thought she was going to tell me which university she'd been accepted for, then for a moment I worried she was going to tell me she was pregnant.

'I'm handing in my notice... tomorrow.'

'Don't blame you, lucky thing, are you going full time at your other job?'

She smiled with a smug twinkle I had not seen before.

'You wouldn't believe how much I'm earning now.'

'Is it banking, your company?'

'Not exactly, though we deal with bankers. Promise you won't tell the others, they wouldn't understand. It's an escort agency.'

I spluttered on my chocolate soaked doughnut. 'Em Ma...'

'It's not what you think, visiting business people like to have company to the theatre, concerts, they don't want to dine alone or if there's a 'Do' they like to take a lady who knows how to behave in company, who can hold an intelligent conversation.'

'So they pay you to be taken to nice places and get free dinners, I wouldn't mind doing that.'

Emma looked at my chocolate covered chin in a way that told me the distance between us was widening rapidly, but had we ever really been friends or just thrown together over the mop bucket?

'But you don't have to sleep with them?'

'Only sometimes...'

That evening I told Mum and Dad about the new revelations, I needed advice.

'Well love, I don't think it's any of your business,' said Mum 'sounds like she knows what she's doing.'

'Don't you get involved,' agreed Dad, as if the vice trade might be catching.

How could I help her if I didn't know where she was living and I wasn't likely to go to places where she would turn up with one of her gentlemen.

Two weeks later we were getting ready for a big family wedding, my older cousin was marrying some posh bloke at St. Andrews Church and the reception was at the Royal Crescent Hotel. The best man lived in Germany, rumoured to be flying in by private jet.

I missed the service. I stayed in the graveyard with my noisy toddler nephew and another cousin whose baby kept crying. At the reception we were on the outer tables; children, teenagers, autistic cousin, uncle who'd had a stroke, lesbian aunty and partner, divorcees and young adults like me who didn't have a partner. We were so busy sorting out who was going to sit where, it was a while before I looked up at the top table. I hardly recognised my cousin the bride as she beamed down on the rest of us. I read the table from left to right; chief bridesmaid's dishy boyfriend, bride's sister, uncle, aunty, handsome groom, bride, groom's dad, groom's mum, best man with cheesy smile, best man's girlfriend... I had to look twice, she was beautiful and she was familiar.

She might genuinely know him, though that seemed unlikely if he lived in Germany. I glanced at Mum, she had only seen Emma once for a few seconds, it was unlikely she would recognise her. At the top table you had to have a partner, perhaps his girlfriend had left him at the last moment, I could see now that escort agencies were quite a good idea and if he lived in Germany no one here would be any the wiser. If we all mingled later... I would pretend I didn't know her, not giggle or blush...

The first dance was over, my cousin wanted to make sure everyone felt welcome, she took me and mum and dad over to chat to her new husband... and the best man.

'Aunty, Uncle, this is Max, they were at Harrow together, but he's living in Germany now and this is his partner Katrina.'

'Katrina' shook my hand, her cool fingers briefly touched my hot sweaty palm; Max put his arm around her waist and swept her away to meet his friends.

I ran after my nephew, chatted to relatives we hadn't seen for a while. In the ladies 'Katrina' was coming out just as I was going in.

She winked at me. 'Thanks Sweety.' Emma talked differently now.

We watched the happy couple leave in their limousine, much hugging of parents, manly handshake between groom and best man, hug and kiss for 'Katrina' from the groom...

'Are you ready to make a move?' asked Dad.

I looked around, but Max and 'Katrina' had melted away.

I never saw Emma again.

Restoration Project

When Ellie Smith went in search of her real family she did not expect to acquire a whole village. Inspired by her favourite programme 'Heir Hunters' and encouraged by her kind, but poor foster parents, who vaguely recalled rumours of money in the baby's background, she avoided the official route and hired a private detective. If she was a lost heiress, she wanted to be found.

Lord Sandford had never acknowledged the existence of his youngest child. Danny Driver, proprietor and sole employee of the Double D Detective Agency, used methods that were unorthodox, but successful. He had obtained a court order for a DNA sample to be taken from the lord as he lay on his death bed.

Lord Sandford's family were no strangers to misfortune and he had outlived them all, including his sons. On a cold February morning Ellie and Danny slipped into the back pew of the little chapel on the Sandford Estate. The gloomy chapel was full of mourners, but the atmosphere was surprisingly light hearted. They were all employees of the late lord, or residents of tied cottages in Sandford Village. When they turned to watch the coffin carried out to the family tomb there was a collective murmur; they saw two strangers and yet some recognised Ellie.

'Miss Ellie Smith?' A man who appeared to be every shade of grey, including his hair and skin, was the only person to approach them as they stood back from the circle round the overgrown tomb. '...and you would be?'

'Miss Smith's solicitor' lied Danny.

He shook their hands. 'Tumbrel, family solicitor to His Lordship; if you would care to partake of some light refreshments up at the house? Then I will have an announcement to make to the gathering.'

'The reading of the will?' asked Danny.

'Not exactly...'

For most villagers it would be the first time they had set foot in the 'Big House', but they had willingly gathered firewood at the handyman's request; it was many years since a fire had been laid in the grand fireplace.

The vicar joined Mr. Tumbrel as he ushered Ellie and Danny up the wide steps to the imposing front door. She was glad of the vicar's steadying hand at her elbow as everyone turned to stare. They parted away from the fire, but not because the girl looked chilled to the bone. The roaring flames licked the ornate marble mantelpiece; above it hung a huge painting with gilded frame. It portrayed a young woman standing by the very same fireplace, though the flames were a little tamer. Above the fireplace in the painting was the very same picture...

'I believe,' said the vicar 'that if you were tall enough to peer closer, you would see the painting repeated into infinity.'

That wasn't the reason Ellie was standing transfixed; the woman in the picture, even allowing for the magnificent dress and hairstyle, looked exactly like her.

'Lady Sandford in the first year of her marriage' said Mr. Tumbrel.

The four of them stood alone by the fire now. The locals were enjoying the buffet and there was a happy hum in the great hall.

They ignored the two strangers as Mr. Tumbrel ushered them to the table. Ellie stood dazed while Danny demolished pies and sandwiches. When the table was bare, the solicitor summoned the gathering to the library. There were a few chairs for the elderly, the others pressed in as best they could. Mr. Tumbrel addressed them.

'I know you have all been anticipating the reading of Lord Sandford's will; hoping he may have had a change of heart and left the estate to the National Trust or English Heritage. The truth is, there is no will. Dr. Williams and myself are witness that Lord Sandford was of sound mind two months ago when, unusually, he asked for a fire to be lit in his bedroom. It wasn't because illness made him feel the cold. With words best translated as Sod The Lot Of Them,' a flicker of a smirk passed over his face 'he requested me to toss the will he made ten years ago into the fire. He had every right to die intestate, I respected his wishes.'

A disgruntled murmur circled the room. Mr. Tumbrel cleared his throat.

'A claim has now been brought to my attention that Lord Sandford fathered an illegitimate child late in life and the business of the inheritance must now go before the courts.'

The muffled sniggers turned to an angry rumble and Ellie felt as if she was in a gothic movie.

Danny stood up, looking nearly as nervous as his client. 'I am representing Miss Ellie Smith, who you see before you.' The historic surroundings had inspired a change in his manner of speech. 'An orphan, fostered since she was a baby, she sought only to discover if she had living blood relatives or perhaps a small inheritance.'

A woman interrupted. 'We don't need no scientific evidence to see she's a Sandford, good luck to her, she'll need it.'

There was muffled laughter and Ellie smiled nervously.

The solicitor turned to her. 'The estate comprises the house, chapel, the village and several working farms, the tenants are naturally anxious. I'm sure this is a sad day for all of us, but the beginning of a new chapter in the long history of Sandford. The members of the household staff will find their Christmas bonus has been paid into their bank accounts, a little late, but that is reflected in the generous amount. Now it is time for Miss Smith to accompany me to my office.'

Mr. Tumbrel drove Ellie and Danny into the town of Sanderton where the offices of 'Tumbrel and Son' were situated.

After a visit to the smart cloakroom Ellie felt a little tidier and more confident. Danny smiled encouragingly as they sat in the office.

'Does your son work here?' asked Ellie.

'No, I am the son,' he replied brusquely 'now to business.'

'Are you saying I'm going to inherit a whole village and real farms?'

'I'm not saying anything until the courts have decided; someone else might pop out of the woodwork.'

But no one else popped out of the woodwork and it was hot and sunny when Ellie and Danny next visited Sandford. She drove her parents' battered car; Danny's business did not stretch to the expense of running a vehicle. Ellie had not yet paid him for his work, but she had promised him a hefty bonus. Her optimism did not last long once they were inside Mr. Tumbrel's office.

'I couldn't find you listed Mr. Driver, are you still representing Miss Smith?'

'Yes he is.' Ellie had practised being assertive.

'Well not to worry, I should be glad to act as solicitor for you and the Estate. First I shall explain in simple terms how things stand and then you can decide if you wish me to assist you in surmounting the many problems. There is no money as such, what little was left has been used paying the staff wages. Lord Sandford spent no money on the estate and thus the estate makes no money. The house is in state of great disrepair...'

'Oh I don't want to live in that horrible old house, me and my parents could have a little cottage in the village.'

'All the homes in the village and on the farms are tied cottages, they have tenants, you can't evict them.'

'Oh I wouldn't do that, I want to be a benevolent benefactor... with an estate manager, as I don't know anything about farming.'

'There is no estate manager, none of them lasted more than a year.'

'I get the impression Lord Sandford wasn't very popular' quipped Danny.

'He was an old man, there were tragedies in the family... he wasn't the young man my father knew, modern country life isn't like the Sunday evening dramas. Have you visited the village yet?'

'No...' In truth, Ellie had been daunted by the thought of the strange villagers.

Even with the sunshine Sandford looked in a sorry state; grass grew out of broken slate roofs, window frames were rotted.

'The estate owner is responsible for maintenance of the buildings, that hasn't happened for years; the tenants have been withholding their rent.'

'I'll donate the whole village to the National Trust, I don't mind living in a caravan in a field.'

A flicker of amusement crossed the solicitor's face. 'I doubt they would want any of this estate, it has no historical value.'

The village looked deserted until a young woman emerged from a shuttered building with a crooked shop sign. Mr. Tumbrel groaned audibly as she approached them eagerly.

'Maisy Dickson, historian, reporter on the local paper, you probably won't remember me, but I was at the funeral. Is it true you have inherited everything?'

'Yes, but I have no story to tell you.' Ellie felt a tide of hopelessness wash over her. 'I'll have to arrange for Mr. Tumbrel to pay Danny's fees, if he can squeeze any money from the estate, then I just want to go home and forget the whole place...'

'Oh but you mustn't feel like that,' Maisy put a sisterly arm round her shoulder 'it's all so exciting, there's so much history here, but I can't get anybody interested. Surely you want to know about the woman in the painting and the rest of your family?'

Danny's eyes lit up. 'My work is not finished yet, more fun than following unfaithful spouses.'

The three young people stood looking at the painting. Danny had opened the dusty wooden shutters and sunlight streamed in.

'Lady Elizabeth Louisa Mary Sandford, you have the same first name. I think the painting could be worth a great deal.'

'Sell it,' said Danny 'and you can mend all the cottages and pay my fees.'

Ellie was alarmed. 'No, she mustn't leave here, this is where she belongs.'

'Oh, have you heard about the legend?' said Maisy. 'Her Lord Sandford decreed it must never be moved, whenever someone has tried... but I'll tell you about that later.'

'That beautiful box her hand rests on, inlaid with gold; I expect she kept all her jewellery in it' said Ellie wistfully.

'Yes, portrait painters always included symbols of family importance; the box shows Lord Sandford's wealth, but the most exciting thing would be to find that box, or the treasures on the mantelpiece.'

Ellie was caught up in the excitement. 'We could restore this room to how Lady Sandford knew it.'

'That would be a dream, but it's the search that is important, to get television interested in her story and yours.'

'Property Restoration, Cash in the Attic,' fantasised Danny 'let's explore.'

They opened doors, found others locked, climbed the stairs...

'All these rooms, but there doesn't seem to be a toilet' shivered Ellie.

To her relief they found a prehistoric bathroom. When she pulled the chain the ceiling high cistern rattled and pipes throughout the house gurgled. Back in the corridor she couldn't see the others; venturing into a blue bedroom she saw it, a small bronze statuette she recognised from the painting.

'Are you okay Miss?' The gruff voice startled her and guiltily she stuffed the ornament into her shoulder bag. 'Only it's not safe to wander upstairs.' She turned to see an ancient crooked man. 'I'm the only one left, I was Lord Sandford's butler... if you and your friends are looking for the box, you'll be unlucky...'

When the other two appeared he seemed to fade into the walls, they followed as she fled down the stairs.

'I feel like a burglar in my own house, did he follow us?'

'Who?'

Before explaining she delved into her bag, then laughed nervously. 'I can't even reach to put it back on the mantelpiece, but at least I've found one treasure.'

'We will find the box,' said Danny 'three more floors to search…'

Restoration Project was first published on Cutalongstory.com

Roast Pork

The smell of roast pork tantalised his nostrils and made his mouth water. It was a long time since he had eaten his sandwiches and his circular route through the New Forest should have brought him back to Hinton Admiral Station by now. But there had been no sign of a railway line, let alone a station; no sign of a road, let alone the comforting sight of a gravel car park with notice boards.

He followed the scent trail, picturing a cosy pub, a hidden gem he could boast about to friends at work. Day One of training for Hampshire Tough Man had not gone well, but perhaps something of the day could be salvaged. Tough Man hopeful had left his smart phone and wallet at home as part of the exercise; he was carrying only a small amount of cash so he would not be tempted into a pub or restaurant. He regretted that decision, but hoped his coins would stretch to a cup of coffee, a packet of crisps and a helpful barman to give him directions.

The trail led him down a sandy slope into the trees, muddy hoof prints by a tiny stream made it an unlikely path to a pub and deterred him from his survival plan of drinking natural water. But hope was revived suddenly with the scent of wood smoke mingling with the roasting meat. The sun emerged from the clouds, sending rays piercing through the new green leaves and revealing coils of white smoke. Two more steps and he was in a small clearing, yards away from a squat building receding into the trees on the other side of the glade. Strangely coloured stones jumbled into walls were propped up by a wooden door and overhung by brightly coloured straw thatch. Tough Man was surprised there was no sign, then realised with a jolt that in such an isolated spot it must be someone's home. They would be unlikely to welcome visitors, but a line of washing, above a small stretch of grass at the side of the cottage, reassured him that this was a family dwelling and he would not have to contend with some suspicious old man.

As he approached, a sweet smell, a blend of pick-a-mix and Lush, overpowered the scent of wood smoke. Stooping to the crooked door he spotted something metallic in the overgrown grass and picked up a mobile phone. He now had a good excuse to knock. The rapper, blackened metal in a shape that reminded him of a hand or claw, produced a muffled tap. As he waited, a flutter of white at the edge of his vision made him look down again. A piece of paper lay on the damp grass, he looked up to see a small square latticed window ajar. He picked up the paper and looked at two scrawled words *Help Me.*

He knocked at the door urgently now, picturing a young mother taken ill, her children helpless. He almost fell in the door when it was wrenched open and was surprised to come face to face with a smiling old lady, dressed strangely, not in denim like his Gran.

'Sorry to bother you, only I found your phone and then this note; is someone ill?'

The phone and paper were in the old lady's hands before he could blink.

151

'So kind of you to bother, I must have dropped my phone.'

'…and the note?'

She ignored his question and beckoned him into a little parlour with a roaring fire, welcome in the chilly spring afternoon.

'You'll have a drink of something warm?'

'Oh yes, a cup of coffee if it's no trouble, then if you can point me in the right direction I'll be on my way… uhm, is that your family calling, grandchild?'

He thought he heard the ceiling creak, though it was hardly credible that there could be an upstairs in such a low house. When the old lady suddenly picked up a red hot poker from the fire, he started back in fright, but she merely plunged it into a pewter tankard.

'Mulled mead, just what you need' she smiled.

He sipped tentatively; it was a comforting warmth and did not burn his lips.

'Delicious thank you; I know it sounds ridiculous, but I have no idea where I am. Are we near Hinton Admiral?'

'Who's he?' the woman looked genuinely puzzled.

He shivered as he felt the first panic rising. How could he have got so lost?

'Perhaps your husband could give me directions.'

'My late husband never gave nobody nothing.'

'How far are we from the A35?'

'Why don't you just enjoy your drink and stop gabbing.'

'I should go now, smells as if your dinner is nearly ready' he stood up shakily, his only desire now was to get out of the cottage and follow the setting sun till he reached civilisation.

'You'll stay for dinner.'

'No...' he stumbled against the wall, which felt alarmingly soft, but when he pushed at the door it wouldn't budge. The old woman had her back turned, stoking the fire as if he had accepted the invitation to stay.

Now the air felt sweet and cloying, his head muzzy. He saw another door ajar and slipped through into a kitchen long and low. Heavy copper pans hung on racks and the heat was overwhelming from an old blackened range. The smell of roast pork was strong, the range with its heavy doors was big enough to roast a whole pig, but he had lost his appetite. The door closed behind him with a muffled thud and he looked around in vain for a window or outer door. He tried to think rationally, but he knew something was not right, everything was wrong. For a moment he thought the whimpering was coming from his own lips, then he saw a small cage beyond the heavy oak table. He crept round towards the dark corner, cautious in case it was an aggressive dog. Suddenly a hand thrust out between the bars.

Roast Pork was first published on line at Bookshop Bistro

Same Time Next Week

'Same time next week then, Mrs. Bennet.'

'Thank you Liam, the borders are looking lovely.'

Liam backed his van carefully down the long driveway, out onto the quiet road, then leapt out to close the large double gates. He was not the last caller of the day, but Mrs. B. liked things to be just so. She paid generously in cash and he worked hard every Thursday; 10a.m. till 5p.m. during the spring and summer months. He enjoyed the work and was proud of the progress he was making; restoring the wide sloping corner plot to the glorious gardens they had been when Mr. Bennett was alive. The house was far too big for Mrs. Bennett, but who could blame her for not wanting to part with the views every window afforded.

In contrast to Mrs. Bennet's home, the house next door had been taken over by a jungle and the only consolation to being increasingly house bound was that Mrs. Bennet only had to see it when her niece drove her to hospital appointments. Old Mrs Cardew was understood to have gone into a home and with her son in New Zealand nothing had been done about the house. Mrs Bennet thought it a pity a nice family had not been given the chance to buy it. Liam agreed; his family for example, stuck in a second floor flat.

With spring growth, next door's hedge was rapidly reverting to its genetic origins; a line of lusty trees cascaded over the pavement. Liam took it upon himself to trim them back, but although the footpath was now negotiable, passers by could not see the abandoned house, even the front bedroom windows had disappeared behind a tree.

The back garden could not be seen from Mrs. Bennet's side and the rest of the strangely shaped plot was walled off from the road six feet below.

When next Thursday came round Liam ferreted behind Mrs. B's shed, the tall solid dividing fence stopped short of the back wall. He felt like a school boy as he slipped next door through the gap. Only an archaeologist or landscape gardener could imagine how this garden had once been. The imploded glasshouse, the green carpet that hid a pond, the leaning shed, the tunnels that had once been paths winding elegantly down the terraces. But there was no sleeping beauty to be found, the brambles that attacked him hid only an old coal bunker.

But the garden itself was the Sleeping Beauty and Liam felt a thrill at the thought of rescuing it, a secret garden, himself a guerrilla gardener. Instinctively he took the secateurs out of their holster and started cutting, appointing a rough and ready compost heap. The shed leaned at a forty five degree angle, but it was stout enough to hide a few tools. Next he peered over the wall, itself hidden from the quiet road by trees and bushes. A ladder propped drunkenly against the apple tree still had most of its rungs, slipped over the wall it would provide access. Excitedly he squeezed back into Mrs. B's garden, selected a few spare tools and placed them in their new hideaway. He would not steal Mrs. Bennet's time, he returned to his work in her garden, but the plans were in place; a brief visit most days when he was out and about.

As spring turned into summer the garden flourished and Liam decided it was safe enough to bring the children, he had found no trace of broken glass or rusty tools that could spring up and hurt them. This was no suburban garden, a lawn mower was out of the question, instead he had scythed the long grass and a flower meadow was emerging.

On his final safety check one Thursday, he decided to push the shed over before it fell. The sunshine revealed something glittering and white, two tiny fangs attached to a skull, a cat's skeleton curled up; he shuddered. How long since somebody had lost their family pet? He was glad to slip back next door and wash his hands in the utility room. Mrs. B's niece had taken to visiting every Thursday, bringing shopping and offering him cakes and tea.

'Thank you so much Liam, the front's looking wonderful and Aunty so appreciates the hanging baskets.'

'Thanks to the home help for watering them every day' said Liam modestly.

'...and the birds are so lovely this year, I suppose that jungle next door is a haven' she laughed.

Liam smiled, thinking of the hidden nests and the wild bird food he had been putting out.

'Mrs. B does not have cats, that's a great help for the birds, did next door ever have a cat?' he asked casually.

'Oh that awful tabby,' said Mrs. B 'always did his business in my garden, even brought a dead bird in through the back door one day. I think the RSPCA must have taken him away when Mrs. Cardew had to go into the home.'

'No one's heard what's happening about the house?'

'We're completely in the dark, council aren't interested as long as the council tax is still coming out of her bank account. I suppose the son in New Zealand must be paying for her accommodation in the home.'

'…well, back to work, thanks for the tea.'

Liam headed down the garden and turned to see the two ladies smiling and watching through the French doors. He carried on edging the lawn, burying the cat would have to wait until tomorrow.

On Saturday morning he suggested his wife Vicki could do the shopping alone.

'The hours I work with the long summer evenings, I want to make it up to the children, take them to the park for some fresh air.'

The children were thrilled to be part of a secret and obediently followed Liam after they had parked the van. Creeping behind the trees and being helped up the ladder were all part of the adventure and they were not disappointed when he led them through green tunnels, warned them not to fall into the pond and took them into 'the cave', a tiny clearing in the centre of the garden. But he was more nervous than he expected, children's voices carried, especially excited screams and he urged them to speak only in whispers.

Even rain did not stop the visits, most of the garden had its own leafy canopy and if their mother wondered why they came home muddy, she was glad they were not cooped up in the flat with computer games. But it was unlikely the children could keep their secret for long.

One Friday night Vicki suggested it would be nice if her husband took a turn at shopping and she would take the children 'over the rec' for a change.

'Fair enough, go to the swings with Mummy tomorrow.'

'But Daddy,' pleaded the youngest 'we want to take a picnic to the secret garden.'

'You're not taking the children to work with you?'

'Not exactly.'

'Daddy, you said Mummy could see the garden one day when it was ready.'

Liam had not recalled saying that, but it was unfair to expect the children to exclude her.

'I don't think Mummy would like climbing over the wall.'

'I think Mummy would like to know what's going on' said his wife.

'Come and get ready for your baths, while Mummy has a nice sit down. I'll tell her all about it when you're in bed.'

Vicki was not as angry as he expected, after he had washed the dishes and made her a cup of tea.

'That's what I would have loved to do when I was a child, I can't imagine my father taking us on adventures. But what about this house?'

'What about it?'

'What's it like inside?'

'No idea, the windows are so filthy you can't see inside.'

'But haven't you ever gone in?'

'Of course not, that would be trespassing.'

She giggled. 'We could be squatters, but seriously, it's a wicked waste when so many families have nowhere decent.'

'I wouldn't blame people who did squat, that's for sure; but we could not, what would Mrs. Bennet say?'

'I expect she would be glad to see the house improved.'

'You would not want to move in, can you imagine the state of it, you're used to this spick and span flat.'

'It's only spotless, because I'm always cleaning up after you lot. I'm not afraid of a bit of hard work. Anyway, we can do shopping in the afternoon. I'm coming with you and the kids tomorrow.'

The children smothered their giggles as their father helped their mother up the ladder. When they were safely inside the wall, they danced around her excitedly, all talking at once, but she forged on ahead, eager to see the house.

'Wait, it might not be safe, I forbade the children to go past that point' Liam whispered urgently.

159

He was right about it not being safe, as his wife tried the handle on the French doors it came off in her hand and as the door started to open, it fell off its hinges, but it was not the shattering of glass that caused her to emit a piercing scream.

Startled, the children mutely obeyed when Liam told them not to move. He took the broken steps to the crumbling patio two at a time and Vicki threw herself into his arms. Over his wife's shoulder he saw her, sitting in a chair looking out at the garden; faded fluffy slippers, a long skirt, several layers of moth eaten woollens around her shoulders, wispy white hair and a teacup resting on her knee. Yellow teeth were fixed in a wide grin and two empty sockets gazed at him.

Sleep Lab

In the comfortable warmth of the theatre I dropped off to sleep soon after the opening discordant chords and woke only when the chandelier plummeted.

'How could you fall asleep during Phantom of The Opera?' complained my husband.

Last week I was late home when I woke up at Terminal Four Heathrow; Hounslow West is my stop on the Piccadilly Line; better than the time I found myself at Slough bus station.

But at home, in our body moulding 'Slumberease' bed, sleep does not come easily. My brain won't switch off, my calf muscles twitch, I resist the temptation to glance at the triumphant red numbers on the digital clock.

Sometimes I fall asleep swiftly, plunging straight into a dream, my mother has come to work with me just as the office walls fall outwards; I wake up in time to avert disaster. The clock says 12.15a.m.

On Sunday night I was really tired after a weekend gardening, bed had never been so welcoming. I sank into the mattress, the clock read 10.59 p.m.

At Green Park Station I dashed through the arch onto the platform, I slipped between the doors as they were closing... but the train had gone, I was falling onto the track...

My body jerked me back into bed.

'I was nearly asleep,' complained Ben 'you elbowed me in the face.'

The clock read 11.00 p.m., I could not get back to sleep.

It was Ben who saw the item in the health pages.

'Sleep Lab, not like Big Brother is it?'

'No, you won't be on telly, it's serious research, it wouldn't do any harm to email this professor; your insomnia's getting worse, you'll be falling asleep at your desk next...'

I didn't like to admit I'd been doing that for years, though nobody had noticed.

'...you probably won't get chosen.'

There was an air of jollity as twelve of us were picked up in a mini bus at the little rural station. We had been requested to bring only a small backpack with our underwear and consent forms; a disparate group, but we soon started chatting.

'I'm bound to sleep better out here, I'm right under the flight path in Richmond.'

'Right over my roof in Hounslow,' I said 'but it's not the planes that keep me awake, when the first flights come in I drift pleasantly back to sleep, then it's time to get up.'

'Exactly, I was fine when we backed onto the District Line, I've hardly slept a wink since we retired to Anglesey.'

'Aren't any of you worried about where we're going,' said a young woman 'I nearly changed my mind when I read that we couldn't bring our phones or our own clothes.'

'Free accommodation and food, en suite bathrooms with fluffy bathrobes and a library full of books, I wouldn't miss this for the world' said an older woman.

When we saw the clean white coats we guessed this was no Warner Country Hotel.

'Looks more like a mental institution' I quipped.

The others had fallen silent.

'Perhaps it's a luxury spa,' said a woman hopefully 'massages and treatment rooms.'

We were ushered into the garden room for tea and biscuits and welcomed by Professor Hallam, also dressed in a gleaming white coat.

'Welcome to Hallam Hall, home to my family for many generations. The modern world is full of colour and noise, here our aim is to provide a simple, calming environment. In your room you will find clothing and toiletry requirements. We will meet in the dining room at six, my assistants will show you to your rooms and collect your valuables to put in the safe.'

More nameless white coats showed us to our rooms, we were separated before we had a chance to discuss what was happening. It was not like the country house I had imagined, no paintings or old furniture, white walls instead of flowery wallpaper.

I was quickly disorientated and glad to be shown into my room. A glance out of the window showed reassuring rolling lawns, but had I been foolish to surrender my watch, purse and return train ticket? There was no clock in the room, I checked the door, it was not locked, but the corridor was empty, best to wait till I was collected for dinner, get my bearings. I sat on the edge of the bed and looked at the selection of books on the bedside table, no titles I recognised.

I must have dozed off; the book I had been reading lay on the floor and I could hear knocking on the door.

In the dining room there was a circular table laid with twelve places, some people had already changed into white track suits. We were served a simple but delicious four course meal by waiters also dressed in white. Each time the waiters retreated we talked amongst ourselves.

'Thought we'd have wine with our dinner.'

'Did you notice there are no numbers on the doors?'

'Has anyone got a television in their room?'

'Don't like the book selection, no thrillers, all science twaddle...'

'No, I haven't seen any clocks either.'

When we adjourned to the library we expected coffee would be served, but we were alone in the room. I investigated the books; they were either written by Professor Hallam or had blank pages. As if reading my thoughts, the professor materialised.

'All done for show, my grandfather presumed most guests would not bother to take a book off the shelves. Please take a seat. As you will have gathered we serve no artificial stimulants, you will find as you unwind sleep will come easily.' He grasped his lapels earnestly. 'But your brain is busy when you are asleep, or should we say your mind is busy while your brain sleeps.'

An animated discussion followed about the difference between mind and brain.

'...so we will monitor your brain waves while you sleep, or to be more accurate, read the energy pulses of your mind. When you wake during the night or in the morning please write what you remember of your dreams.'

Back in my room, my mind was whirling, I hadn't used my brain this much since science A levels. The assistant put two small patches on my temple.

'I thought I'd be wired up, sensors all over my head' I joked.

'No, it's all done digitally these days' he replied solemnly.

Knowing I could just turn the light on and read without disturbing Ben, no clock, no alarm to worry about; I slept soundly all night. In the morning I found it hard to put into words the kaleidoscope of people and places in my dreams.

The day was filled with guided walks through woods in full leaf and by the lakeside. In between we attended scientific talks. After the evening meal we were given our first assignment; to plan dreams set in the grounds we had visited.

In my dream I waved to my father who stood on a jetty on the other side of the lake. I set off along the muddy path, dodging branches, but however far I walked, I could not reach the other side of the lake.

'Excellent,' said the professor, as I described my dream to the others 'you directed your dream, but incorporated previous experiences. Why do you think you could not reach your father?'

'Because he has been dead for four years.'

'And would you like to reach him?'

'Yes.'

'So tonight you plan a way to cross the lake.'

I enjoyed listening to the variety of dreams that could take place in a wood, but at lunchtime a few people complained.

'What has this to do with insomnia, more like psychoanalysis.'

'I don't believe he's really measuring our brain waves.'

At dinner there were only ten of us, but Professor Hallam was unperturbed.

'We want only people committed to the project, tomorrow we take a big leap of imagination and understanding.'

I concentrated hard as I drifted off to sleep and I was soon rowing across the lake. I tied up at the jetty and my father held out his hand to help me up. We had a nice chat, every day stuff. I did not mention he was dead, nor did he.

By the way Dad, I always meant to ask you...

Before I could ask, I was back in bed.

The meeting was straight after breakfast, we faced a television screen, the first we had seen. There were nine of us. As Professor Hallam spoke I realised it had never been about insomnia, but that didn't seem to matter. The lectures we had attended, the books I had dipped into, all began to make sense as he talked eloquently. My brain had never felt so receptive.

'A simple question that I try to answer in my book "In the mind of God", what is reality? Did your dreams feel real? The artist imagines a picture before he paints, the film producer pictures his movie in his mind. Did The Creator imagine the whole universe before he created it? You cannot see radio waves or electricity, but you know they exist...'

It was hot in the room, I was beginning to lose concentration, I wasn't as clever as I thought I was, Hounslow was where I belonged, not in the outer reaches of the universe. He was still talking.

'...different wavelengths, other dimensions, there is no limit to where our minds can wander. I shall now prove dreams are not just in your own brain, you give them a physical existence.'

The screen came to life, we saw the sun dappling the leaves of the woods, I saw myself walking. We had been filmed. A strange woman walked into the clearing, one of the men gasped. On the screen he ran towards her. In the room the man cried out. 'You've taken my dream' and lunged towards Professor Hallam.

As the assistants held him back I saw myself on the screen, chatting to my father, my chair toppled backwards as I stood up and stepped towards the television. But my scene faded and a bear leapt out of the bushes to attack the woman sitting next to me; she screamed at the same moment as her screen self let out a terrified cry.

The woman attacked by the bear was not at lunch, there were only five of us at the table, before dinner we had to decide whether to leave or sign up for another session tonight.

'I was so close,' said the man who had run towards the woman 'I have to try again.'

'I do not need to try again, my father is dead, I have no right to disturb his peace or will it just be my mind I am disturbing?'

'The only thing I'm worried about,' said the older woman 'is will I be able to get to sleep tonight?'

Solar Power

Something flashed by Daphne as she hobbled painfully onto the patio. With her macula degeneration she could only tell that it came from the house and headed for the end of the garden.
Hopefully it was a neighbour's cat, not an urban fox or rat; whatever it was, it seemed unlikely the dog had summoned the energy to chase it out.

Wiggy the Jack Russell had been a retirement present to her husband and the tireless dog had encouraged them to walk miles across the downs and through the woods. Now it was a struggle for her or the dog to get into the garden. The frustrating thing was, her mind was sharp as ever, but she shouldn't grumble, better than being the other way round. Now her youngest grandson had come to live with her, she had plenty of mental stimulation. She hardly saw the other five grandchildren; busy, busy, busy, contracts abroad, house shares in the city. Jason was regarded as a bit of a nerd, probably on one of those 'burger syndrome spectrum' things, but what was wrong with being highly intelligent and not wanting to go clubbing? He reminded her of what her father must have been like as a young man before her capable mother took him on as a challenge.

Jason looked out of the top floor window, hoping the dog hadn't escaped. The jungle at the end of the two hundred foot garden hid a dilapidated fence. More worryingly, had Gran seen Wiggy racing by? He hadn't explained his latest experiment.

Selling solar power was the latest of many unsuccessful part time jobs taken to fund his masters degree. It had sparked him off on yet another tangent to his main studies, but this time it had become his quest.

He genuinely believed everyone should take advantage of the solar panel installations, primitive though they were. It was criminal to waste a limitless source of free power, but most householders feared they could not afford the outlay, the actual cost was the only information Jason was not allowed to put across.

He could not even persuade his bosses to install free solar panels on Gran's roof. A survey revealed the old Victorian house was unlikely to fall down of its own accord, but nor would it survive any interference.

Jason dashed down two flights of stairs, through the French doors into the garden, where Daphne was putting food on the bird table. Thanks to the solar powered squirrel scarer they had many bird visitors.

'Something shot out of the house Jason.'

'I know, I'll go and investigate, check it wasn't a fox.'

In the undergrowth he was in time to see a cat flee through the fence towards him, pursued by Wiggy; he grabbed the dog with a rugby tackle and removed the cap. The dog wilted in his arms. To avoid explaining how the ancient, arthritic Wiggy had got there, he squeezed out through the same hole into the back lane, made his way round to the front of the house and returned the dog to its basket.

Breathless, he arrived back on the patio. 'Must have been the neighbour's cat; you sit in the sun while I put the hoover round.'

The rambling old house would have defeated even a lover of housework, but as part of his experiments, Jason didn't mind. Besides, no one in the family believed he could look after himself, let alone his grandmother and he was determined to prove them wrong.

His uncle would be quick enough to get the house sold to pay for a care home and that would be a tragedy. The old house was ideal for his experiments, not to mention free board, but most importantly it had been his great grandfather's house and the attic was full of his long forgotten notebooks and equipment. What others regarded as shell shock from World War One, Jason knew to be genius.

When the solar kettle had boiled by the back door he took a tray out into the garden.

'Coffee's ready, I'll just bring the vacuum cleaner out to charge.'

'Is Wiggy okay?'

He had forgotten to check the dog and was relieved to find he was still alive; the success of the experiment was beginning to sink in.

'Shall we go on E Bay when I get back from uni?'

'Oh yes, it's so addictive, only one more box of stuff to go.'

They had hit upon an ideal way to keep the house clean easily, get rid of all the ornaments. Daphne announced to the family last month that she wanted to share out the valuables while she was still alive; bring a cake on Sunday and take your pick she had told them. In truth, not much appealed to anyone and she and Jason had been delighted to find that even the ugliest items were valuable to someone on E Bay.

Jason spent a rewarding afternoon at the research centre with his loyal band of undergraduates; his field of study was the human brain, so they made ideal guinea pigs. He could not do to them what he had done to the mice, rats, real guinea pigs and Wiggy, but they did enjoy being scanned and studying brain waves. They were thrilled to hear about Wiggy's success and Cassandra presented Jason with the human version of the cap she had crocheted for the dog.

It was beautifully made, with the photo cells threaded into the intricate pattern like shiny beads. Any lady would be pleased to wear it and would not look out of the ordinary when she went out and about, but though Jason would have loved Cassandra to wear it and she was keen, he was a professional.

That evening, as they ate their Indian take away, Daphne wanted a research up date; it did not all go above her head.

'So the brain is full of electrical impulses, the sun is a giant power station full of electrical energy. Your solar panels can power a house, so a solar hat could power a human being?'

Gran had got to the heart of his theory much quicker than he'd expected, would she suspect when Cassandra brought the hat round tomorrow?

Daphne didn't believe all that electrical stuff, but she loved to tease Jason, have a laugh. 'That's the thing I miss even more than my eyesight, or joints that work... I used to have so much energy. But you wouldn't want to waste your inventions on me, what about the Olympics? That would give the other countries a surprise.'

Jason joined in the joke, though he did have a strange expression on his face. 'Don't you think the other athletes would notice if they had solar panels on their heads?'

'The swimmers could hide it under their caps' she chuckled.

'Gran, we are going to have a visitor for coffee tomorrow.'

'Oh, one of the chaps from university?'

'Yes, well she's a girl, Cassandra, one of my research students.'

This news was far more exciting than her grandson's experiments and she was in good spirits as she hobbled upstairs to get ready for bed.

Jason set up the bedside giant kindle, said goodnight to his grandmother, then went down to tuck Wiggy in. The poor old dog closed his eyes; each night Jason wondered if he would wake up in the morning and how Gran would cope if he didn't.

'Another treat for you tomorrow old boy.'

The next morning the sunny weather continued and Jason brought Cassandra out onto the patio to meet Daphne. The girl was much prettier than the old woman had expected... hoped, though her clothes were a little strange, but as she only had peripheral vision it was hard to be sure.

'Hello dear, are you as brainy as my grandson?'

Cassandra blushed. 'None of us are and my family just think I'm weird.'

'So do Jason's… I mean I'm sure your parents are very proud of you, studying science. You'll have to excuse me if I seem to be staring sideways at you, it's my sight.'

They all sat enjoying the pleasant weather; Wiggy and the vacuum cleaner were brought out to soak up the sunshine.

'What a nice bag dear, I love bright colours.'

'Yes, I made it myself, I make all my own clothes… actually I made you something.'

Daphne peered closely at the colourful, crocheted hat, feeling the intricate pattern. 'It's lovely, shall I try it on or save it for winter?'

'Wait, cried Jason in alarm… I mean save it for winter.'

'I suppose you're going to tell me it's a solar hat.'

'We do have a surprise for you, Cassandra made Wiggy a hat as well.'

When he took the tiny hat out of his pocket the dog's tail wagged feebly. Jason slipped it on, easing his pricked ears through the two holes. Wiggy's tail wagged furiously, then he ran round the patio in circles. Cassandra was as surprised as Daphne at the instant effect.

'Even in the shade or indoors the charge lasts for a while,' said Jason proudly 'but we mustn't leave it on for long, we don't know what the long term effects might be.'

'What does that matter,' said Daphne 'he's enjoying himself. Are you trying to tell me my hat would have the same effect?'

'It works on mice, rats, guinea pigs and dogs, but the human brain is so complex… and it would go against all the rules.'

'Hang the rules; think of all the things my father wanted to try and didn't.'

Suddenly Wiggy raced into the house and returned with his lead in his mouth.

'Well I never, that lead has been hanging in the hall for a year untouched, I didn't want to move it in case I hurt his feelings.'

Wiggy looked pleadingly at each of them.

'Shall I take him for a walk?' said Jason.

'Perhaps I'll come as well.'

Nervously he handed her the hat and she pulled it on snugly, stood up and clipped the dog's lead on. Before they could protest Daphne was at the front door; out she walked with a spring in her step.

Solar Power won third prize in the Balsall Writers' Short Story Competition 2012.

Summer Delight

When Vinny saw the pictures he wanted to leave, this old bungalow was not abandoned. He made his way into the dark hallway, peeped through a half open door and signalled frantically for Sam to come out; there was a shape under the covers, a person asleep. If Sam wouldn't leave he would go without him, as quickly and quietly as possible. But before slipping back out through the French doors he took another glance at the paintings, luminescent in the moonlight; no one but his friend would think of doing a burglary at full moon. Inside the frame street lamps turned the rain into needles of silver and the autumn leaves into gold, car headlights made the wet road shine; the painting was called 'Autumn Lights'. On the other wall 'Summer Delight' by... he couldn't read the signature, didn't dare pause longer... a hand clapped him on the back.

'Let's get out of here,' said Sam 'lucky he didn't wake up.'

ooo000ooo

'You must be mad George,' said his carer 'meeting victims, hearing offenders apologise, fine, but inviting him to your home for a fortnight...'

'It's a challenge, Vinny seemed genuinely sorry, scared almost.'

'First name terms already?'

'He can do some hard work, better than a young offenders institute, I think I can help him, he's got talent and when he sees you…' the old man laughed 'he's just a skinny kid, he'll be more scared of you David than we are of him.'

Vinny didn't know why he had said that; usually sullen, when he was nervous words just came out of his mouth. He could go picking up rubbish with Sam or spend two weeks doing housework for the old man. When he heard the man's name he knew the paintings were his. In his mind's eye he saw the seaside scene, pinpricks of light dancing on the rippled turquoise sea, coloured triangle sails on the horizon. Then in the foreground, on the beach, a father with his toddler at the water's edge, the little boy laughing as wavelets covered his toes, you would swear the water was moving. The shallow sea was clear, how had the artist painted clear with solid colours? In the bottom corner the scribbled writing 'Seaside Delight by G.R. Appleton.'

'Could you teach me to paint, Mr. Appleton?'

Vinny had said the right words, his social worker looked pleased and started ticking boxes, mumbling about positive attitudes.

'I can see you're good at drawing' said the old man.

'I love drawing, but I want to learn to paint, paint in colours.'

At the meeting the boy had not sat with his head bowed over his mobile phone screen like most youngsters; his mobile had been confiscated at the door. Instead his head was bowed over the form they had each been given to fill in, boxes to tick, comments to make. The boy didn't write, he drew obsessively, lively figures dancing round the page.

ooo000ooo

When Vinny knocked nervously on the door of Mr. Appleton's ramshackle cottage on Monday morning, he was taken aback to be greeted by a huge bloke with biceps bulging out of a bright turquoise polo shirt. Across his prominent pectorals were stretched red embroidered words 'Care West'.

'I come here three times a day and I'll be watching you; all the drawers are locked and Mr. Appleton doesn't keep valuables in the house. You're very lucky he agreed to take you on, he's not a well man and I don't want you getting him stressed.'

The only person getting stressed is me, thought Vinny. The young man led him into the room with the paintings, the old man was sitting in a chair with a table over his lap.

'Good morning Mr. Appleton'. The social worker had been giving him lessons on manners.

'Is your real name Vincent, like the artist?'

'What artist? Only Mum calls me Vincent, I hate it.'

'Okay Vinny, what do you want to do when you leave school?'

'I've already left, unofficially.'

'Did you do art at school?'

'A bit... could you teach me to paint like that?' Vinny looked round the room, there were paintings on every wall.

'No. I can teach you techniques, but you will have your own style. The only brush you are going to hold this week is a six inch decorator's brush; if you and your mate thought this house was derelict then the outside must need painting.'

'Okay, where's the paint?' Vinny knew there would be a catch, but house painting sounded more fun than housework or gardening and if he got it done today he could be in front of an easel tomorrow.

'Preparation is important for artists and workmen, first you have to sand down the woodwork... now let me introduce you to David, my carer, or perhaps minder would be a better description.'

It was hot work. David brought him out a glass of water before he went on to his next client. 'There's an outside toilet, no need for you to go in the house.'

'Isn't there any Coca Cola?'

'No, I'll see you when I come to get Mr. Appleton's lunch.'

Vinny wondered if he'd get any lunch.

At one o'clock the boy was summoned to the back of the house where a few broken paving slabs passed as a patio. Mr. Appleton's wheelchair was perched precariously near to where the garden sloped

179

steeply down to the wall Vinny and Sam had climbed over.

'What a glorious day,' said the old man 'I suppose you would rather be down on the beach on a day like this.'

'Nah, the beach is boring.'

'When I was your age, during the war, I would have given anything to live by the seaside, even holidays were out... beaches covered in barbed wire and land mines.'

Vinny thought it wouldn't be long before the war came up. The old man was eerily good at reading his mind.

'Well, you don't want to hear about the war. Let's go for a walk after lunch, you can wheel me along the promenade.'

At the cliff top Mr. Appleton decided they should go down in the cliff lift. 'I don't trust your driving down the cliff path.'

On the promenade Vinny began to get the hang of the wheelchair, but hoped he didn't see anyone he knew. They paused to enjoy the view, the boy perched on the wall; all the benches were full of other old people taking in the sun. It was going to be a boring afternoon.

'This is your first lesson Vinny, what do you see?'

'Hey, this is just like your painting, 'Summer Delight'.

'Yes, it was a day just like this, I wanted to capture it for ever, but the painting's all I've got left...' George paused, the boy wasn't listening and the man wasn't sure if he had spoken the words out loud, wasn't even sure if he had nodded off for a while in the heat. He took a ten pound note out of his wallet. 'Go and get us an ice cream, I haven't had one for ages, not supposed to with my diabetes.'

'Is that why you can't walk?' Vinny was relieved to hear him talking again, for a moment he had wondered if he had quietly died. He decided to keep him talking.

'No, got all sorts of things wrong with me, paying for my past sins.'

Vinny wondered what the sins might be, it would be rude to ask, but now he had started talking he wanted to ask lots of questions. 'If you're very ill why did you take me on, do you trust me with that money, I could just walk off and leave you.'

'Yes and you could have pushed me over the cliff top, or you and your mate could have stabbed me in my bed, but you didn't. Perhaps I would have deserved it. I need to atone for the past.'

The old man was rambling. Viny wondered if he was mad.

'Why did you break in to my house, do the other things?'

'I dunno, bored...'

'I did far worse when I was your age, during the war.'

'But you couldn't have been bored, in London, being bombed and all that, I bet it was exciting.'

'It was, for we boys, but we did some bad things because we could get away with it; our dads away, the blackout... Billy was the leader, we followed, but that does not excuse us. He kept daring us to do more, once it went badly wrong; if that was in the news today everyone would be shocked. No one found out; we fled and soon after there was an air raid, the house was flattened by morning. I've never told anyone this before. It all comes back when you're old, I can't undo the wrong.'

Vinny didn't know what to say; part of him wanted to know exactly what happened, though he couldn't imagine this feeble old man doing anything wicked. He was not used to grown ups talking to him about serious things.

They ate their ice creams in silence, then George continued as if only seconds had passed.

'Get yourself an honest job, go to college, learn to be an artist... but don't get sucked into anything bad; walk away, like you did that night at my house. I sometimes wonder if things in my life were sent as a punishment... Okay, sermon over, back to the art lesson.'

'I can't do scenery, only people.'

'Lots of painters do scenery because they can't do people. Watch everything that's going on, that toddler digging in the sand, the couple holding hands, children splashing in the waves. Now let's go to the so called art gallery.'

Ten minutes later Vinny awkwardly manoeuvred the wheelchair into the small gallery full of holiday makers.

'They're not half as good as your pictures' he whispered.

The gallery owner frowned as George talked in a loud voice. 'Flat, no life, no light. Your figures have such life, now you must play God and create a world for them to live in.'

By the time David returned to get George's tea and help him to bed, the painting room was scattered with pencil sketches of people, dogs and seagulls.

ooo000ooo

By the end of the week the window frames and French doors were painted a bright blue, but indoors no paints had appeared. Vinny had taken George out in fine weather every afternoon, but on Saturday morning it poured with rain; David and Vinny climbed up in the tiny loft and fetched down mysterious boxes.

Soon the battered old dining table was scattered with tubes, tins, assorted brushes, but no paper or board. Vinny was shown how to mix colours.

After lunch the wind blew the rain away. To David's disapproval Vinny wheeled the old man down to the sea front. They looked at the muddy grey waves and beige foam. George laughed.

'If you can capture the colour of that sea, then you are a real artist.'

'There are still people to paint… and dogs.'

'Windswept holiday makers, fed up children, could you capture all this in a picture?'

The boy laughed 'I'm going to call it Summer Delight.'

ooo000ooo

183

By the end of the second week a painting stood on the easel, Vinny had opted to try oils. The social worker was talking to the boy out in the garden and David was examining the work of art.

'It's not finished yet, of course,' said George 'but I think it's pretty amazing, it's got movement and light.'

'Better than some of those pictures at the gallery; your challenge was a success, turned a thief into an artist.'

'He was never a thief, he's done his two weeks, but we'll only know the challenge has worked if he turns up next week and the week after, if he wants to keep learning.'

Summer Delight was first published in An Eclectic Mix Volume Two AudioArcadia 2015

Up, Up and Away

She had suggested the picnic. He was touched, not many girlfriends… dates, potential girlfriends might be more accurate… had taken an interest in his job. Flight Engineer impressed them for a while, until they realised it did not involve aeroplanes, but Louise had a sense of humour. When he had asked about her work she had replied modestly that she was stuck indoors all day with computers.

He had met her at his brother's barbeque, now she had agreed to come down to Sandbourne on the train. He replied promptly to her email.

No need to bring a thing, I'll supply the picnic, or Marks and Spencer's will.

XX Guy.

He deleted the last line.

Look forward to seeing you, Guy.

Louise liked flowers, that was a good start, she was delighted with Sandbourne Jubilee Park. The council had won an award for small town gardens, Guy was not sure if that referred to the size of the town or the gardens. Sandbourne also came third in the regenerated resorts competition.

'I love August' said Louise, as they walked from the renamed Beach Plaza into the cool of the gardens. 'Look at those zingy oranges and lemons, they only open their petals when the sun shines, that makes them all the more special.'

Guy saw everything anew through her eyes and wondered if this was love or just hope. He offered her a spot under a tree, where the grass was still soft and green, in case she liked the shade.

'No, I want to sit near the flight zone, see the action.'

He led her through the dappled pergola for maximum impact.

As they emerged she exclaimed in surprise 'Oh, it's bigger than I expected.' She read the large writing, red on a white background. 'S.S. Sandbourne, sponsored by Red Alert Accident Insurance.' She giggled '…and does your big balloon have accident insurance?'

'No need; it can't burst, we don't fly her in bad weather and we can bring her down in a flash if there's an emergency – though we never have one.'

'Let's sit here on the grass, better leave the bench for that old couple. It's like velvet' she said, as she settled gracefully.

'Yes, Gordon, head of Sandbourne parks nursery, is very proud of his lawns, it breaks his heart that people are allowed to sit on them.'

'I'm glad we are, what a perfect day.'

Guy was glad Louise appreciated life's simple pleasures, he did not earn a lot as assistant flight engineer and he did not want a girlfriend who liked clubbing and shopping. They ate crayfish sandwiches, a change from his usual cheese and pickle, as he explained the operating procedures.

'So when it's ready for take off we undo the guy ropes; my mother must have had a premonition when she named me.'

Louise laughed, new listener to an old joke.

'But what keeps it attached to the ground?'

'The cable, tensile steel, hundreds of separate wires, the same as the cables on suspension bridges.'

'But how is the cable attached to the ground?'

Guy was thrilled that Louise was taking an intelligent interest. He suppressed the image of Brian, gung-ho owner of Sky Skimmers Ltd.

If the public knew there was only one nut and bolt between them and the wild blue yonder...

'The securing device is weighted in a ton block of concrete' he reassured her.

'Oh my favourite cakes, how did you guess...'

But the idyllic picnic was not destined to last; a large family settled a few feet away. Guy and Louise smiled in the common greeting of those enjoying lovely weather, he was feeling magnanimous to all humanity in her presence and she was naturally friendly. They grabbed the blow away carrier bag and the roll away ball, but their cosy picnic chat was hampered by their new neighbours. The five children came in different sizes and sexes, but all had penetrating voices.

'When can we go in the balloon Daddy?'

'When you've eaten your lunch.'

'But I'm not hungry.'

'You said we could have fish and chips Mummy.'

'They'll be no fish supper if you don't behave and eat your lunch' replied the mother in a grating voice.

'Where does the balloon go Daddy?'

'Higher than the trees, higher than all the buildings in Sandbourne.'

'Then where?'

'It doesn't go anywhere, you look at the view then come down again.'

'I… want… to… go… over the sea to A Nother Country.'

'Don't be stupid' said his brother.

'But you said it was a hot air balloon, it hasn't got any flames, it's boring.'

'I hope they're not having a ride the same time as us' giggled Louise.

'We won't go till they've had their ride and I hope that's soon; she's on the way down now.'

That was when Guy had his idea. He turned to catch the parents' attention. 'Sea mist starts rolling in about half an hour from now, you might be wise to catch the next ascension.'

'You been up there?'

'Yes, I work at the flight base, day off today. Views are fantastic, along the promenade, right across the bay.'

'Is it scary?' said a child.

'Oh yes.'

'Bet it doesn't go up high' said the tallest child.

'It does if they let the cable out to the full length,' lied Guy 'I'll nip over and have a word with the flight engineer.'

'Shall I keep an eye on your bags?' asked Louise.

'Oh thank you' said the mother, gathering everyone up.

Guy strode importantly over to talk to Wesley, the Chief Flight Engineer, who had been working with the balloon for less time than Guy, but was a nephew of Brian the boss.

'Oh Guy, just the man, could you have a look at the moorings, I heard a bit of a clunk earlier.'

With the huge cable reel hiding the mountings it was impossible to see if anything was wrong. The family were already stepping into the round basket, directed by the passenger assistant, their voices piercing the air.

'I want to go that side.'

'It doesn't matter where you stand, idiot, it's round.'

'Oww... Dad, he hit me.'

Guy stood up. 'You're the boss Wesley, you know the emergency procedure, if anything looks amiss on the ascent, bring them straight down.'

'Who's the pretty girl then,' asked the other man, his concern for the mountings forgotten 'going to take her for a ride?'

Guy smiled smugly and settled back on the grass with Louise.

'I like children, but not those ones... I hope you won't be bored, you must have been up thousands of times.'

'No, I'm ground staff, the important job; the ones in the red uniform are just ticket collectors.'

'That breeze is nice and cool, we'll lose the shade now she's going up.'

They gazed up, shielding their faces from the sun, the voice of the commentary floated down.

To the south you can see the remains of the Edwardian Pier, soon to be restored with a lottery grant matching the large donation from Red Alert

Accident Insurance. To the north the splendid Victorian building, originally the home of the Sandbourne Science Society, now houses the offices of Red Alert Accident Insurance, the friendly local...

The voice of the commentary faded away.

'Looks like your friend is letting the cable out to the max' said Louise innocently.

Guy stood up suddenly, then sat down as quickly; he was not on duty.

It was Wesley's lack of attention to duty that saved his life; he wandered away from the base to answer his mobile phone. A loud crack disturbed the peace of the gardens, a second louder noise was at odds with the silent ascent of the balloon. The frayed end of the thick steel cable missed Wesley's head by inches as it whipped round in serpentine fury.

Louise dropped her plastic glass of wine, Guy stood up shakily, the Chief Flight Engineer stood clutching his mobile phone as if unsure what to do with it. They were joined by others staring up in awe at the vertical ascent of the balloon. No one was sure if the faint cries came from the passengers or surprised seagulls.

Wesley's fingers hovered over his phone. 'What's the emergency procedure?'

'There isn't one for this situation...' replied Guy, the summer colour draining from his face. He heard random voices around him.

'Is it a helium balloon Daddy?'

'Call the police.'

'It will come down eventually when the air inside cools.'

190

'Not the police... Ministry of Defence...'

Guy could not take his eyes from the tiny white dot in the azure sky, someone was shaking his arm and talking to him.

'Guy, your friend's lost it, you'll have to phone... now, the Ministry of Defence, tell them it's urgent, use my phone.'

The phone was already ringing as her cool fingers placed it in his hands, his tongue felt thick in his mouth as an important sounding man answered. Louise motioned to the orange wind sock that pointed towards the sea. She mouthed words.

Wind direction, tell them the wind direction.

The conversation finished and he looked up to see several bemused police officers.

'He's called the MOD,' Louise addressed a sergeant who stepped forward 'there's nothing more we can do.'

'We'll be the judge of that Miss.'

'What can the MOD do?' whispered Guy.

'Shoot it down,' she spoke between clenched teeth 'hopefully before it comes into contact with civil or military aviation.'

Guy sighed with relief. 'That's okay then, no air bases around here.'

She shook her head in despair. 'We're on a major flight path here.'

'But it will come down too quickly, what about the passengers?'

'One dreadful family or hundreds of airline passengers? It's probably too late for them.'

Guy wished this was all a nightmare, the picnic ruined and Louise... he tried to pull himself together.

'How do you know all this stuff, the MOD phone number?'

Her teeth chattered, the shock beginning to set in made her words come out as a giggle.

'Like you, I hardly ever fly, I just work in the control tower at Heathrow.

Xmas Eve

Linda hated Christmas, or rather the long run up to Christmas. It was busier but easier when the children were still at school; they knew exactly who would be there for Christmas every year; four children and four elderly relatives. Now, since the children were grown up and the elderly relatives no longer around, each year was different.

But this year would be the first Christmas she and Roger had spent by themselves. He was looking forward to spending Christmas Day and Boxing Day alone, relaxing; Linda was not. With the prospect of such a quiet Christmas there did not seem to be anything to get ready for, so she didn't.

It was quite liberating, others talked of vast amounts spent, huge crowds fought through and piles of presents waiting to be wrapped. It only took Linda one afternoon to buy the requested gift vouchers and post them off. On the food front Christmas Eve would be no different from her Saturday morning shop at the local butchers and greengrocers.

But the day before Christmas Eve things started to unravel. She checked her emails in the morning and there was a long one from Sarah.

...remember the English guy I met at the backpackers' hostel? (no she didn't) *Well, we're an item now! Unfortunately, his visa has nearly run out so we are trying to get a flight home together...*

In the afternoon John rang, he thought they might be lonely and had swapped shifts; he was getting a lift home on Christmas Eve.

In the evening Kate called; Gavin's parents had found a last minute booking on the internet and were off to spend Christmas in the sun; she and Gavin should be down by tomorrow evening, picking up Paul on the way. Hadn't Paul told them he'd broken up with his girlfriend on Tuesday?

Linda looked around the house; apart from the cards, there was no evidence of the festive season. Roger was completely calm, though disappointed he wouldn't be having his quiet Christmas; he was already working out when they would go again.

'They can take us as they find us, they know we weren't expecting them.'

He reluctantly went up in the loft to bring down the decorations and lights, but Linda's joy at having a proper Christmas was tempered by her panic at how much there was to get ready. She thought of the small joint of pork on order at the butchers and the miniature pudding in the cupboard.

'No problem,' reassured Roger 'we're finishing early tomorrow hopefully, in the morning you just have to make up the beds and make a shopping list; we'll go and do a big shop when I get back.'

It took Linda a long time to get to sleep that night; when would Sarah arrive, what was the new guy like, would the weather be okay for Kate and Gavin's trip down or would they be involved in a massive pile up on the Motorway, why hadn't Paul told them of the break up?

The next morning Roger decided to take the bus to work as parking would be horrendous, but assured

Linda he would be home by two o'clock. She rushed around with piles of bedding and towels, tidying, dusting, vacuuming; she was enjoying herself, but at one forty five the phone rang. It was Roger.

'Sorry darling, I'm going to be late, all hell's broken lose here, I could be very late, lucky I left the car at home, you go ahead and do the shopping without me.'

Terror gripped Linda, surely he wasn't expecting her to drive to the shops?

'But Roger I…'

'Sorry dear, got to go, see you tonight.'

She looked out of the front window at the shiny red car leering smugly at her. Officially Linda drove; she had a licence gained at the second attempt, a spotless licence with no points. When was the last time she had actually driven? She had certainly never driven the new red monster Roger had bought when their other car packed up. *Take it out during the day when it's quiet, it's lovely to drive* he had said. How Linda envied those people who proudly stated *I never learnt to drive* or who remarked *I don't drive* as if it was an incurable medical condition. Had she ever enjoyed driving? She couldn't remember; parking, turning right, roundabouts had always presented problems. With the first baby she had ventured out with him safely strapped in the back seat, but he had started crying and she could not concentrate.

She realised she much preferred the healthy option of pushing the Silvercross pram; you could get loads of shopping in the tray underneath. They had never been able to afford two cars, so much of the time the car was not available for her to use. Roger enjoyed driving, on outings and holidays he naturally slipped into the driver's seat.

As the children got older and had to be taken to things it was difficult to avoid; but they soon realised it was embarrassing being out with their mother. People would be tooting as she held everybody up, trying to get in or out of the multi storey car park or they would have to walk miles to avoid awkward parking places.

When they all learnt to drive confidently they gave her lifts; otherwise she was happy walking, cycling, going on the bus or accepting lifts *Roger's got the car, such a nuisance!*

Now there was no getting out of it. She could never bring all that food home on her bike. Where had Roger put the car keys? Linda hunted all around the house then found them in the pocket of his spare coat. She knew you pressed the button to unlock the car; that was all she knew. Opening the front door she looked round to make sure nobody was watching, slipped into the car, then slipped out again to open the gates. The road was busy and the driveway sloped down steeply, another reason she was loath to use the car. Linda turned the key and the engine started, but her mind went blank till she remembered it was automatic and managed to get it into reverse. For the next ten minutes she blocked the pavement as she waited for a gap in the traffic.

When she finally lifted her foot off the brake pedal she rolled straight back into the opposite kerb. Somehow she got into forward gear and set off to the sound of angry beeping from the car she had just missed. She perched on the edge of the seat; it was set well back for Roger's long legs.

Linda had forgotten the new roundabout and stopped to work out which exit she wanted, an impatient horn tooted behind her and she set off in panic, missing her exit and going round again. As she drove up the new dual carriageway she dared to feel a little confident. The brilliant lights of the supermarket loomed ahead, she was going to make it. But where was the entrance? Not over the footbridge or through the cycle underpass; all she could see were hedges and fences. After circumnavigating the whole superstore complex she hit upon a solution and followed the huge supermarket lorry.

Linda was pleased with herself as she drew into a nice quiet car park and found a large bay. She locked the car but as she walked away a loud rough voice yelled out and she realised he was addressing her.

'Hey you stupid…'

Linda could hardly believe the words she was hearing. She turned to face a scowling driver climbing down the four steps from his cab.

'Do you want me to crush your… red toy car, move it now.'

As she shakily got back into the car she stalled twice and finally backed out, cheered on by sneering trolley boys. The main car park was busy, yellow jacketed figures directed drivers into impossibly small spaces; she squeezed in, clipping the wing mirror of the next car. The only way to get out of this terrible place would be to shop slowly and leave after everyone else had gone.

Shopping slowly proved easy as it was so crowded; her trembling hands pushed the wonky trolley, the only one left. Little children cried, school children skidded down the aisles and arguing couples blocked the junctions. She was tempted to abandon the trolley, the shopping, the car and just walk home. When everyone turned up at the house she would announce that Christmas had been cancelled. This get out plan comforted her a great deal, gave her the confidence to try just one more aisle, then another; gradually the trolley filled up and it seemed a shame to abandon it. The long queue at the checkout reassured her; the car park should be empty by the time she got out and in the dark nobody would see her.

At last she was outside, but could not remember where she was parked. In the dark the red car was not so bright and shiny.

A security man came over 'Can I be of assistance Madam?'

'Well you won't believe this, but I can't remember where I put my car.'

'I certainly would, it happens all the time,' he replied kindly 'now what is the registration number and make of the car?'

All hope disappeared; she couldn't remember the number and didn't know the make. Her brain had switched off when Roger had talked interminably about what car to get; all she had been interested in was how much it was going to cost.

'Red you say Madam, how about that one over there?'

He gallantly steered the uncooperative trolley over to the car and she hoped he would not witness her attempts to drive off. Luckily his radio buzzed into life. She struggled to get all the shopping in the boot and wondered if the car would get back up the driveway, weighed down so. The cars either side had gone and she followed other vehicles to the exit.

Linda recognised the nice quiet little road at the exit, she cycled on it to avoid the main road; the circuitous route through the residential area would be safer. She noticed the dashboard for the first time, or more specifically the petrol gauge, it was nearly on empty. Had Roger mentioned filling the tank up? Yes. Would she pass a petrol station? Would she know how to use the petrol pump? No. There was only one thing to do; get home as quickly as possible before the petrol ran out. When she heard the police siren she pulled over carefully to let it pass and was surprised to see the police car stop in front of her.

'Did you know this is a twenty mile an hour area Madam?'

As she looked into the face of the law in the light of the street lamp a wonderful thought occurred to her; if she got lots of points on her licence maybe they would take it away.

When she arrived home a car was blocking the driveway, but she didn't care if she left the red monster on the main road. In the light of the street lamp she saw the boot of the strange car was open and beneath it Gavin, Kate and Paul were hauling out huge bags of shopping.

'Hi Mum, we knew you wouldn't have much in, so we did a big shop on the way.'

Xmas Eve was first published on line at Bookshop Bistro

About the Author

I have been writing frantically for nearly ten years; taking it seriously when I joined a weekly writing group. One of my weekly short stories turned into a novel which turned into the trilogy, but I have never stopped writing short stories. It was the writing that propelled me into the ether; I still put pen to paper, but becoming a self publisher has involved a steep learning curve.

As fast as we authors learn to connect with readers and writers, some new form of social media arrives. Writing and real life come first, in that order, but social media can be fun if you just do the parts you enjoy. As well as writing blogs myself I enjoy reading and commenting on what other writers have to say for themselves. Writers' Facebook groups are also a great way to meet authors from all over the world, though I haven't yet connected with anyone from North Korea...

It is at this point, at the end of the book, that lots of writers beg the dear reader to write a review. Don't worry, I would not dream of suggesting that, I just hope you enjoyed the stories. If you do happen to be on line with a few minutes to spare, wander over to the Amazon site where you ordered this book in the first place and write a couple of sentences to tell other readers why you loved or hated it.

You are welcome to visit my website
www.ccsidewriter.co.uk

Read about the other books I have published.
Catch up with my regular Beachwriter's Blog
illustrated in colour.
Enjoy Fiction Focus.
Dip into Travel Notes from a Small Island.
Try the picture quiz.

ooo000ooo

I have published four novels and two short story
collections on Amazon Kindle.
Visit my Amazon Author page.
https://www.amazon.co.uk/Janet-
Gogerty/e/B00A8FWDMU

ooo000ooo

You can find me on Facebook here.
https://www.facebook.com/Beachwriter/

ooo000ooo

I am one of the authors at
www.goodreads.com
where I write a regular blog 'Sandscript' and
also review books.

ooo000ooo

I also scribble a little as Tidalscribe on
Wordpress.com
https://wordpress.com/posts/tidalscribe.wordpress.
com

ooo000ooo

I am a member of
www.thewritersroom.co.uk
Visit to ask authors questions or make
comments.

20896360R00126

Printed in Great Britain
by Amazon